Azarius Borealis is a new upcoming author from Scotland (born 5 Jan 1992). He wrote the supernatural fiction novel *Paper Snow* – his first ever novel. Azarius uses his creativeness to journey his readers into a different dimension, where we do not only uncover the lives of his characters, but also discover parts of ourselves we never knew existed.

Dedication

In loving memory of my best friend, Nicole Ross, who sadly passed away in 2015.

Azarius Borealis

PAPER SNOW

AUSTIN MACAULEY PUBLISHERS™

LONDON • CAMBRIDGE • NEW YORK • SHARJAH

A CIP catalogue record for this title is available from the British Library.

ISBN 9781528905886 (Paperback)
ISBN 9781528905893 (E-Book)

www.austinmacauley.com

First Published (2018)
Austin Macauley Publishers Ltd™
25 Canada Square
Canary Wharf
London
E14 5LQ

WRITING this book has been one of my biggest challenges of life, and it wouldn't have been possible without the support of my close circle of friends and family. A lot of the elements in this book actually relate to my own spiritual journey; some of the characters represent different parts of myself—some parts stolen from an early age, and others I'm just beginning to uncover. This book is for the black sheep, the outsiders, the ones who are told that they are too different for the world. I want all those people to know that being different isn't something to be ashamed of; being different gives you the advantage to create something new in the world, something unique—*Paper Snow* was mine.

Chapter One
Emergence

WHAT does 'the colour *white*' say to you? … I'm pure like sheets of snow; scattered on the highest mountain tops—climb me if you dare! Close your eyes, purse your lips, and exhale all of the air from your lungs onto me; let my fragments dance in the wind as I grant your wishes like a dandelion, plucked from the soil. Pick up that axe; that same axe you used to slay all of the demons from your past, swing it into my cold body—crack me open, and I'll show you my icy depths.

'White' was the colour of my home back then; I didn't go outside much after the accident—in fact, I couldn't remember the last time I saw anything other than those white walls. I felt something *different* inside me back then; I was a prisoner of my own mind. My only visitor, Dr James Coal; Coal liked to study me, he always tried to get to the root of my problems. Now I know, those roots were deeper than we both thought…

Coal secretly admired the Scandinavian interior—I'd catch him observing the walls like a pondering artist. I used to wonder what images he'd paint in that deep dark mind of his. I wanted to run my fingers through his hair, grab his soft black strands tight—tight enough so I could bash his skull against the wall. I wanted to open his head; unravel his mind as it poured down those shiny, white walls. I would find it difficult to make eye contact with him; his eyes were these massive black holes, they would pull me in, and empty the scattered fragments of my mind like tiny jigsaw pieces. My messy mind wasn't 'the problem' though; fitting the pieces together was, and I was a difficult puzzle to solve—even for Coal.

Coal, and I would sit by the window; I'd stare out into the green acres that circled a very special tree—the baobab tree. I named it 'the tall tree' because it was the tallest of them all—growing nearly as tall as the white garden wall. I would get lost in that green paradise all day; the smell of the fresh grass, and the texture of the crumbling bark on the trees. I would watch the unpredictable dance between the wind and the leaves of the branches—spirals of emerald fireworks as both elements collided.

"What's on your mind, Noah?" Coal asked. He could tell I was in a trance as I watched nature work its magic. I could hear Coal scribbling on the pages of his notepad as he observed my behaviour.

"I can't remember how or when we met," I replied, scratching my forehead; I thought if I scratched hard enough, all of the answers might fall out.

"Are you okay?" he asked. I could remember the expression on his face; he looked at me as if I was this unstable time bomb that was about to explode in front of him. I replied with a yellow smile; I used to think my thoughts would be too much for him to process.

I remembered a dream I had the night before that morning; a surreal blur of vibrant flames in the distance, followed by the mumbles of a strange man's voice. I couldn't remember his face—all I could remember was his dark silhouette. I remember being unsettled by that dream in the beginning; apparently, I was so disturbed that Coal's visits were compulsory—they became a regular occurrence.

"Was it that dream again?" Coal asked. It was as if he could see me replaying my dreams over in my mind. "Do you remember this time?" he asked again. It always felt as if he was more interested in my dreams than my physical health.

"I wish it were clearer, I just can't remember much of it," I replied while shaking my head. I looked over at Coal; he was still scribbling in his notepad, I'd hoped he would dismiss my forgetfulness, and change the subject. I used to wonder what he'd write about me; if he thought I was completely losing my mind—I was.

"Maybe you should start writing your dreams down?" Coal smiled at me. "It's a good way of telling your unconscious mind that you listen to it." I didn't know it back then, but now I know that he couldn't have been any more accurate. If I could go back in time, I would've listened to my dreams much sooner.

"Yes…" I replied, in deep thought—I was glad that our minds were on the same wavelength. As complicated as our minds are, usually there is some logical explanation behind our dreams; something that relates to our waking lives—how we think and feel in that moment of time. Sometimes things happen to us that can't be explained because they defy the laws of logic, but that doesn't mean they aren't real. Even now I believe scientists are as close to understanding dreams as they are to understanding the afterlife—we are but tiny grains of sand in this universe.

"Is there anything else on your mind, Noah?" Coal asked. I could tell Coal wasn't interested in anything other than my dreams; his pen stopped after he changed the topic. Coal was a very odd specimen like myself, only more contained. I possess this wondering mind that could jump across oceans of imagination, and forget there was another human beside me—trying to communicate.

I always wondered about Coal; what kind of life he lived outside his profession—could he switch off from the lives of others? He always seemed so calculated; I tried to imagine him in situations where he'd let his hair down. I would imagine—try to imagine—him in different scenarios, but my mind would find it difficult to picture anything other than him being at work. Coal was a workaholic; that was obvious, he was with me almost every day. I would wonder what brought him to those moments with me; the calculated counsellor who wanted to talk about my dreams.

"I feel different today…" I told him, there was something *strange* about that day; I felt it from the minute I woke up. I wanted to tell Coal; but telling him, I felt vulnerable and doing so would only prolong his visit—I wanted to make an attempt to leave that room. I wanted to explore the other side of the room which had the window, and breathe in the fresh prana.

Coal frowned at me, "Define different, Noah?" I struggled to answer him in the beginning; I couldn't remember much of my life before those first few days with Coal.

"Different than the first," I told him; I could remember the panic I felt when I woke up surrounded by doctors that very first day. Coal placed his pen and notepad by the window, then went to fetch a glass of water from my state-of-the-art water dispenser.

"Remember to keep yourself hydrated and eat plenty fruit," Coal told me, before handing me that glass of water. "It's important you keep your vehicle healthy," he said as he opened his black leather briefcase. He pulled out an apple, and placed it in my hands; a forceful reminder to stay healthy. I always wondered how many items he could pull out of his case—it seemed to hold an endless supply of apples.

"Thanks!" I replied, before biting into the delicious red apple. I remember always feeling unsatisfied; my diet always seemed to consist of water and fruit. I would always have a craving for something more—something that would feed my inner carnivore.

"Well, I guess that's it for today," Coal said. "We'll continue again soon?" he asked, gathering his belongings. I remembered how lonely I felt after he left that day; I couldn't handle being alone with this mind of mine—especially one with no memories of the past. "Rest now," he whispered, patting my shoulder before he left the room. I knew I had to find a distraction from my busy mind—colour to the empty white walls.

After he left that morning, I stood in front of the window that faced out into the garden. I remember my eyesight refocusing, as it shifted back and forth towards my reflection. I remember finding it impossible to identify myself; my skin was so white, I almost blended into the walls behind me. My tired brown eyes sat in baskets of blackness above my defined cheekbones. I looked unhealthy.

I would try to reassure myself in that moment; pretend that I would recover eventually. I hoped that my memories would soon come back to me, and I could start to live my life again. I didn't realise that, in that moment, my life was never really mine—it belonged to *them*.

I made my way towards the main door, and placed my hand upon it; it wasn't just any old door, it was a large white door that felt like a metal material. The door had a touch-screen device by the handle; controlled by finger recognition. I remember trying to work out how to open it in the beginning; I remember the frustration when the device on the door wouldn't recognise my fingers.

That was the first time I heard the *strange* sound; chimes coming from my bed across the other side of the room. I remember how relaxed they made me feel—I would fall asleep instantly.

I followed the sound towards my bed where I found another device attached to the ceiling above my white-dressed bed. Another peculiar device with a blue ring light that moved clockwise. I was hypnotised by the sound and the movement of the light; I fell into my white sheets—leaving reality behind.

I remembered the feeling of comfort as a child, as I sunk into those warm white sheets; a faint memory of my mother stroking my face whilst I fell asleep in her arms. The feeling of comfort became more vivid when I saw her apparition leaning over my bed. I wanted to talk to her, but I was stuck in a state of sleep paralysis; my body was stiff and the only thing working in that moment was my wondering mind. Her long brown hair bent onto the bed as she leaned closer towards my paralysed body.

"Sail, Noah," my mother whispered as she glided her hand across my white sheets in a wave-like motion. I tried to reply but my mouth felt as if it was wired shut. Her apparition became distorted as she faded into the beams of sunlight that lit the gathered dust around the room. I wiggled my fingers just enough to wake me from my sleep. I lay there, trying to process what I'd just witnessed.

I remember trying to comprehend that hallucination—I had so little memories of my mother and the rest of my family. I wondered about the last time they visited; I couldn't remember seeing any of my family after the *accident*. As I was becoming more awake, that unsettling feeling I felt from the minute I woke up was coming back to me; my intuition was telling me that something was wrong.

I scuttered around the room looking for paper—desperate to record that moment. After searching the entire room, I was ready to let it go—until I discovered a box filled with paper and string beneath my bed. I couldn't write my dreams without a pen, but I knew I could string them up; a learnt skill from my childhood embedded in my brain—origami. I began to fold and tear the paper until my creation was completed; there it was—a paper boat.

Chapter Two
The Imperfect Butterfly

IT was time to let my dream set sail; I had to look for a place to store my perfect little paper boat—a reminder of my lucid dream. Before I found that place, I lay on the cold white marble floor; placing my beautifully crafted paper boat beside me. I remember my mind sailing into the reflection of the boat as it illuminated against the pearlescent surface. In that moment, I was the captain of my own dreams.

One thing I learnt about myself in those past few days was that I had a thirst for knowledge. My intuition told me that I would figure everything out in time; I found a relief in that, my intuition was the only thing I fully trusted then. I turned over onto my back to face the ceiling; I realised the chimes had finally stopped—I was in complete silence.

"Where did you come from?" I whispered to myself; inspecting the advanced construction of the device. I remember Coal telling me I had suffered a serious blow to the head as I carefully pulled myself off the floor. Back then I had to trust his words; trust that my recovery was a work in progress—even though I barely knew him.

The sunset looked incredible that evening; my face was lit in shades of gold as I approached the window with my roll of string and paper boat. The window was a large glass square that could open as a door into the circular garden. That was the first time I remember opening it; I can still feel the air as it filled my lungs with nature's oxygen—so pure.

I remember how the strands of grass bent beneath my bare feet as I took my first steps into the garden. The rooms were built into the large, circular white wall like a giant sugar doughnut.

The garden was enclosed in the centre of the construction; a well-maintained plot of nature, stretched from each window, all the way to the tallest tree in the centre like an emerald carpet.

I'd always felt this strong 'connection' with nature; it was like it knew I was on its side from the beginning. The garden welcomed me with open branches; the flowers had blossomed and the apples on the trees were ripe—ready to be eaten. When I made my way towards the tallest tree, I was captivated by its height; the tree was a tall tower of endless branches that grew into the warm, open sky above.

When I reached the bottom, I placed my right hand onto the brown trunk that grew from the soil, mentally scaling the climb. I grabbed onto the first branch and began to ascend slowly and carefully. Five or so branches up felt high enough to catch the rest of the sun melt into the earth as it set for another day. I was dazzled in the twilight; the sun ignited the horizon in shades of pinks, and blues. I wanted to stay up there in that moment forever; appreciating nature's display of art.

When the darkness finally approached, I used the last of the sunlight to thread my paper boat to the string. I used my teeth as scissors to cut the string, and tie it around the thick branch above me. As I made the knot, a unique looking butterfly landed on my boat, and I noticed a strange pattern on its wings—an imperfect symmetry. It was as if the universe was trying to tell me something in that moment; it felt as though time had stopped as I watched its wings flutter in slow motion before flying into the air again. I was a caterpillar back then, an empty shell, waiting to remember again—waiting to become the butterfly.

My boat sailed into the wind below as I let go of the string—a reminder of the apparition. When I climbed back down onto the grass below, I left my origami anchored to the tall tree before making my way back inside. On the way back to my room, I noticed that all of the windows were made of dark tinted glass from the outside looking in—including mine. I felt unsettled; not by the thought of someone else watching me, but of me not being able to see on the other side of the glass. I remember wondering what characters could be standing on the other side; ones I would know nothing about, unless they made themselves known. There were exactly six windows spread out around the entire complex; six neighbours whom I had yet to meet.

As I went back inside, I noticed a basket of red apples sitting by the door with my name attached to it. I remember walking past them; I left them by the door before heading straight into the shower. All I wanted that night was to feel water on my skin; I had been neglecting myself since the accident. Since most of my memories had been erased, the only thing I could think about in that moment was my mother, and how her hand sailed through my sheets like a boat. I wondered where she was in that moment; wondering when I'd finally see her face again.

I thought about the first day I woke up after the accident; I remember how confused I was, scared out of my mind and my only natural response was to fight. I couldn't even think about what had really happened to me—part of me wasn't ready to know the details. The only person who seemed to care for me then was Coal; if it weren't for him I would be even more lost.

After showering that night, getting myself to sleep was a struggle; I would purposely try to keep my mind wide awake. I kept having that same dream about the shadow man, whispering to me beside the fire. I would lay awake in the dark, holding onto my head, hoping to stop the fear from spreading around the room. I had so many questions and so little answers; my only quest was to find them—I was a unique jigsaw piece picked from the grand puzzle. All I had to do was find the missing links; but, as it turned out, those missing links were looking for me too.

Chapter Three
The Tall Green Time Travellers

THE first answer was given to me on the third night, I just didn't know it 'back then'. I remember the fourth day like it was yesterday; how the sunlight shimmered over my bed sheets as dawn approached—inviting me to rise with it.

I walked towards the window, and that's when I saw her—the girl who led me to the truth. Looking back, I remember how free she looked that day; the way she observed every plant in that garden, like she'd never stepped outside before. That was the first time I'd witnessed anyone else out there, and the first time I stopped feeling so alone in the world.

Her long white hair grew for miles; tones of shimmering silver sparkled as the light of the sun reflected off the back of her head. She stopped under the tall tree where I'd noticed one of the branches had been broken off. I remember how she knelt beside it and placed her hand over it like she was grateful it had fallen; we both were—I just didn't know it then.

She looked up at my paper boat, still sailing on the branches above her; I could tell she was curious by the way she tilted her head back and forth. She was like a mermaid emerging from the ocean to catch a glimpse of a boat sailing through her waters for the very first time. Before I could swim towards her and introduce myself, she had shapeshifted into a monkey; scaling the tree like a fearless acrobat. I knew that by going out there I might startle her—so I hesitated.

Branch by branch, she made her way up towards my paper boat; carefully pulling it towards her. I remember how the sunlight lit her curious little face, and her expression as she tried to figure out its construction. I went to open the window again, but was greeted with a hand on my shoulder. When I focused into the window's reflection I caught Coal standing there behind me.

"Good morning, Noah," Coal interrupted me. When I turned my body towards him, that was when I realised that even the sunlight had no chance of finding its way down those black holes that lay beneath his thick bushy eyebrows. His eyes were like the night; a night with no stars or moon—just a dark cloudy overcast.

"Why can't I remember what happened to me?" I asked Coal; I was scared to hear about the suffering I'd been through, but at the same time I knew I would be relieved that his answers might give me some peace of mind. He smiled, removed his notepad from his black leather briefcase and placed it on the small white table by the window. He was carrying the same black leather case as the day before, and wearing the same white overalls. White seemed to be the fashion there; everyone, including me, was dressed in white. The only difference between Coal and myself was his name badge, titled Dr J. Coal.

"All I know is that before you were brought home, you suffered a serious head trauma after hitting your head last week," Coal told me. "My job here is to help you regain your lost memories," he continued, staring out into the garden. "It's important that we take things easy for the foreseeable future, so I hope you weren't thinking about climbing that tree out there," he grinned.

Remembering the accident was like trying to open a locked door without knowing about the existence of a key. By losing your memories, you lose your identity—that was the part I struggled with the most.

"Your memories will come back to you Noah!" Coal tried to reassure me before lifting his notepad. "So, tell me, did you have another dream last night?" he asked while slowly opening his notepad. My intuition told me that Coal was keeping information from me; always quick to change the subject, the only thing he was interested in was my dreams.

I was becoming frustrated with Coal. There I was, the twenty-six-year-old man with no identity, and all he wanted to discuss was dreams—my dreams. I decided from that day onwards I wasn't going to tell him about my dreams until he told me what I wanted to know about my life.

"No, I don't remember," I lied to him, knowing he'd work it out after breaking his eye contact. I turned towards the window and noticed that the girl was gone; the curious mermaid had returned to the depths of the imaginary green ocean.

Coal snapped his notepad shut, "Okay, Noah, we can try again when you feel more focused," he said. He made me feel like I didn't want to cooperate for the fun of it, but his reverse psychology didn't work on me. Before he left, he placed an apple on the small white table. After he closed the main door I went out into the garden; making my way towards the tall tree. I could feel my feet sink into the cold soil beneath the grass with every step. There was still no sign of the girl—just an empty green circle.

When I approached the tree, I noticed that the window next to mine had been left open, slightly. I shouted over, hoping the girl would reappear. "Hello?" I yelled over, nervously. I waited for a few moments, but the only reply was from the birds as they fled into the sky above.

My first memory didn't come back to me whilst I was sleep, it came to me in that moment—with my eyes wide open as I touched the broken branch at the bottom of the tree.

EIN

A memory, of my six-year-old self, came flooding back to me like warm summer heatwaves—each wave filled me with childhood nostalgia. This one tree in particular, felt like home, a living entity—my guardian. I saw myself sitting on its branches and as I opened my hands, my eyes lit up when I revealed a sparkling white rose.

The rose began to count to ten in German: "Ein, Zwei, Drei, Vier, Fünf..." Before the rose could finish, I found myself standing in a circle of ten trees. The voice sounded familiar—a young female voice that I couldn't fully identify. "These trees have witnessed many things throughout their lifetimes," the rose continued. "If you listen really carefully you can almost hear them talking to each other!"

I closed my eyes as the wind rustled the leaves on the trees that surrounded me. I came to realise that she was talking sweet sense into my wondering mind. The trees had been here long before us, they'd become the wisest—tall, green time travellers.

In that moment, I was beginning to feel more human again; relieved that my memories were finally coming back to me. The voice from my memory was right; that tree was my friend. I thanked it before making my climb.

Chapter Four
Carbon Copies

UP on the branch of that tree, I found myself contemplating my life again. I noticed the leaves above me came to life as they danced without any wind; the tree was alive and reacting. On the branch, a leaf broke from the twig—like magic it gently spiralled downwards. I was completely focused on its descent all the way down into the hands of the girl who returned once again to the tall tree.

Her eyes were like an electric ocean; big, blue pools filled with innocence and wonder. I could get lost in them all day—I was magnetised. She was wearing a white dress, and already we had something in common; no shoes.

"Lost your shoes too, huh?" I asked her, realising I hadn't been wearing any shoes since I woke up after the accident. She looked up at me, confused like she didn't know what shoes were. I was surprised I did, not being able to remember much else. I began to climb back down to greet her properly, she was much shorter than me, my guess was that she was around twelve or thirteen years old.

"I'm Noah," I told her.

"Aurora," she replied, holding onto a silver locket she was wearing around her neck.

"How old are you, Aurora?" I asked.

Aurora looked into my eyes and I saw something hidden within hers; a great sadness, I knew because I saw it too in my reflection the day before.

"I can't remember…" she replied, almost embarrassed that she couldn't remember. It was like we had both experienced something traumatic, both trying to figure ourselves out. The loneliness of my first days here began to disappear quickly as I found the similarities between us.

"That's okay, want to hear something funny?" I asked her again, hoping to distract her and make her smile. "I can't even remember yesterday," I continued. She looked down at the ground and I realised I wasn't making her feel any better. "I noticed you're a very good climber!" I told her, as I placed my hand on the bark of the tree, admiring its beauty. "Maybe when you make your own origami you can put yours up there too?" I asked with a smile.

Aurora lifted her head to the thought of learning something new. When you lose your memory, learning anything new is like gold. I wasn't sure of Aurora's story back then, but I knew she was suffering just the same; we were like carbon copies of each other.

"I don't have any paper," she replied, I heard fear in her tone. "I tried to get some before, but the sleepers wouldn't let me," she continued.

"The sleepers?" I asked, puzzled by what she meant. I didn't want her to feel worse than she already was; even the mention of it scared her. She ran back towards her window before I could ask her anymore questions. I wanted to shout after her, but the thought of making her more scared terrified me even more.

I walked back to my room, even more confused than when I left it. I left my paper boat up the tree, hoping that we'd cross paths again. Looking back now, I wish I never let her run away like that. I felt protective of her, like an older brother wanting to protect his younger sister.

Meeting Aurora for the first time reminded me of how frightened I felt when I woke up in my room surrounded by strangers in white jackets. I'll always remember the fear I felt the morning after the accident; it was like being born into the world, except I had full awareness, just no memory of anything before.

That day I was becoming restless, pacing around my room trying to remember anything I could. I started bashing my head with my palms, hoping that I'd knock some memories back into my brain. I had found another way to be productive—keep my mind focused.

I found some courage and grabbed the apple that Coal left behind, and made my way towards the main white door. As I placed my hand on the device, I heard those same chimes from the day before and followed them back towards my bed. I couldn't remember much after that moment, except the sound of the apple hitting the floor as I fell into my bed and the voice from my memory repeating itself.

"Hurry, Noah!" I followed the voice towards the tree from my memory and fell into complete darkness as the ground opened up.

Chapter Five
Icy Depths

INTO the black abyss I went, my soul was consumed by complete darkness. During that moment it felt like the end. I prayed to myself, hoping that someone or something was listening to me. I used to think I was special, unique—that it was me against the world that sleeps. I used to think I was this 'chosen one', someone sent to Earth to awaken humanity. In that moment I realised how small I was in this vast, endless universe. I felt powerless and I surrendered, I surrendered to the blackness that consumed me.

The Snowflake

ANOTHER memory came back to me like a cold winter breeze, freezing the orphanage windows. A grand fireplace burned under a Christian cross, keeping the orphans warm as they filled their bellies with soup and bread. All of them gathered on the floor, wrapped in blankets and sharing their pasts and there was me; my seven-year-old self, standing by the window.

"Why don't you come and join us, Noah?" One of the older ladies asked, trying to encourage me to keep warm with the others. I wanted to be cold though, I wanted to turn to ice that day, standing by the window. Even though it was Christmas Eve, I just wanted that window to shatter before me and turn my skin blue. Why was I so sad? What had happened to

*me? I didn't even acknowledge the kind woman trying to keep
me safe and warm from the cold.*

*I placed my hand against the icy glass window and closed
my eyes. In that moment I whispered to myself as the snow
began to fall on the other side of the window. "Come back to
me...come back." I open my eyes again and caught the descent of a snowflake. My eyes widened, amazed as the water
molecules create this six-fold hexagon crystal is it fell before
my eyes. This was the first time I'd witnessed the sacred ge-
ometry in nature. A tear escapes and falls down my face as
the snowflake disappears and melts into the white abyss.*

*"Things are going to get better, Noah," the lady whis-
pered into my ear as she wrapped a blanket over my cold
body. "Nature is a beautiful thing you know!" she told me,
"we are all part of the cycle, like the leaves that fall in au-
tumn...they fall from the tree, but new ones grow in their
place," she continued, drying my tears before she pulled me
towards her.*

I was thankful for that memory, and how it reminded me that
even falling into this black abyss I was still a part of this great
cycle. Everything that was happening was happening for a reason, even if I didn't know the reason yet. I let go of all fear in
that moment and finally my fall came to an end as I crashed into
a pile of snow—just like the snowflake.

A small fire lit the darkness and I fell into another familiar
dream. From the midst of the flames, the shadow man appeared,
running over to me in cold desperation.

"IkKumak!" he shouted as his feet crunch through the snow.

My breath turned to smoke as the heat from my body bursts
into the cold air. "Help!" I whimpered from my trembling icy
lips.

The shadow man pulled me up towards him, his face still in
darkness but I could make out the fur on his hood as the fire lit
his silhouette. "Sua?" he asked, pulling his hood back so I could
see his face properly. I could tell he was Inuit by his Asian features and Eskimo fur-apparel. His skin like dark oak and eyes
like the night sky. His moustache was tangled in tiny shards of
ice and his wide mouth carried a deep voice of authority—but

who was he commanding? I heard others like him talking in the background.

"English?" I asked nervously, hoping that we'd break the language barrier.

"Yes, some!" he replied. "What is your name?" he asked slowly, trying to get his words right.

"Noah," I replied, "What's yours?" I asked him, shivering against his fur coat.

His eyes lit in surprise at my name, he turned around to gather his tribe. A woman and her child walked towards me, both wearing similar fur coats. He turned back towards me, smiling. "My name is Aput!" he said. "Here Aput means snow," he told me as the woman handed him a flask.

"Where is 'here', exactly?" I asked, confused and cold. Aput placed the warm flask in my hands, encouraging me to take a drink. The warm coca filled me with warmth as it poured into my body.

"You are in the Arctic, my friend," he told me. Both the woman and child knelt down beside me. Aput pointed to them both and told me, "This is my family, Ahnah!" pointing to the woman, "and this little one is Uki," he said, pointing to the girl who was holding onto her mother.

Ahnah had long black hair that trailed from her hood down to the bottom of her fur coat, strands frozen from the cold exposure. Uki had her mother's face, beautifully defined features, and dark oak-skin, like Aput. I felt a deep warmth from them; a welcome into their tribe.

"I...don't understand, how did I get here?" I asked.

"We found you buried in the snow, along with your backpack," he replied. I looked around to see white bricks surrounding us, realising we were inside of an igloo.

"Go!" Ahnah told Uki, who ran outside to fetch my belongings. I felt my eyes beginning to close again and grabbed Aput's hand, squeezing it tight.

"Noah?" I heard him speak to me, trying to keep me awake. Uki came running back inside with my backpack, but my vision became blurry and they faded back into the shadows as I woke from my sleep again.

Chapter Six
Restless Shadows

I emerged from my sleep; my mind in overdrive as the dream replayed over in my mind. I realised how long I'd been sleeping when I looked over to the window, the sun was descending, and I wanted to use the last of it for my recreation. I rolled onto my side, pulled my white sheets with me and let the blood drain to my head as I looked beneath the bed for more paper.

The marble floor glistened as the dying sunlight reflected against the white. I spotted the sheets of paper beside the apple I'd dropped earlier that day. After mentally preparing myself, I grabbed the sheets of paper and tried to visualise the snowflake from my memory. Origami was a learnt skill, one I hadn't forgotten somehow.

The tree was becoming my memory bank—a reminder of my dreams. Up I went with my paper snowflake, my second reminder. I hung the snowflake on the branch above my paper boat. Darkness finally arrived, and I could hear the sound of footsteps, trailing through the grass in the garden below.

After making my way back down from the tree, I looked around expecting to see someone, hoping Aurora had returned. There was nobody to be seen but I could still hear footsteps amongst the trees in the distance. I called out, hoping whoever it was would reveal themselves, "Hello?" I stopped hearing the footsteps and everything was silent for a moment.

From the midst of the shadows, further in the distance, a mysterious figure appeared, wearing all white. The mysterious stranger stood and watched me for a moment and then disappeared behind the trees again.

"Wait!" I yelled, hoping they would hear me. I ran towards the end of the garden, desperate to catch them. I heard the sound of a window close and when I got there, the person was gone. They could have disappeared into any one of those windows as they all looked completely identical with dark tinted glass. The last thing I wanted to do was harass a stranger, so I made my way back to mine.

On the way back, by the tall tree, I noticed something reflecting in the grass from the light of my room. Something that I would've noticed earlier, something that had to have been dropped by the stranger. I remember feeling unsettled during that moment, wondering how I never spotted them earlier, this person was stealthy.

There it was, the first clue to who had been lurking in the shadows earlier—a small pen titled 'C.O.C' inside a circular logo. I was oblivious that night; the truth was everywhere, and I didn't even know. I kept a hold on the pen and made my way back inside where I thought I would feel safer.

I knew something was out of balance on that fourth night; my intuition knew that something was wrong and no matter where I went, I wasn't safe—especially in the darkness. I closed my window shut, and wrapped myself inside my white bed sheets. Under those sheets was my only comfort during that night, I felt so lost and confused. All I could think about was the whereabouts of my family and why my mother still hadn't made any contact with me. I began to wonder if she even knew where I was in that moment.

Trying to recover my memories on my own was impossible. I didn't know it back then, but there was another force at work—a pattern that took me a while to figure out. I didn't sleep easy that night, my mind was in overdrive and I lay awake for hours, wondering about my life.

Hours passed and it was getting late. Finally, I was surrendering to the fight against sleep; I could feel my eyes becoming heavy, my eyelids relieved as they rested over my eyes. Even though I was exhausted by my own thoughts, my eyes didn't stay closed for long, they were opened again only moments after. My heart pounding; almost too frightened to move when I heard a loud thud in the garden.

Chapter Seven
The Strange Lady

THE fourth night had other plans for me; the universe wanted me to be awake more than ever. Time didn't exist to me back then, I had no way of checking; no clocks, no phones and no computers. Technology was forbidden, and there was nothing to distract me—that was the only way they could get us to listen.

Back then, the only thing I knew was fear; fear of the past and not being able to remember anything. I was scared of what the future might hold for me—terrified of the unknown. I remember getting out of my bed that night after the thud. I had no way of protecting myself of any danger, nowhere to run; even if my brain went into flight mode, I had to be brave—I would have to fight.

Outside of my window I saw another thick branch, beside the other that broke the night before. Another mysterious figure stood by the broken branches, completely naked. I didn't know what to think or do, I found it hard to believe at first. Their flesh like candle wax, white and shiny as the moonlight painted their body from above. The mysterious person was facing the tall tree—marvelling at its beauty.

There was something empowering about that moment, and the fear I felt earlier was gone. This tree was also connected to this person, and that person felt it too. They worshiped the tall tree and raised their hands into the sky like branches growing from their flesh. I heard them thanking it and dancing around it, and that's when I noticed it was an older woman. She looked so happy out there, so enchanted by nature—in that moment, she was free.

When the strange lady disappeared into the night, my anxiety disappeared as well. I was surrounded by others who felt this intense connection with nature, and I was beginning to find a strange comfort in that. I wondered about my neighbours for the remainder of that night; both Aurora, the fearless acrobat who also felt connected to the tall tree, and the naturist, who graced me with her bare flesh. We all had that one connection in common, and I felt connected to them because of it.

I lay awake that night, waiting for daylight to arrive again, and when it did, so did Coal. He was different on the fifth day, more apprehensive. He looked as if he didn't get much sleep either, the night before, and kept pacing around my room from wall to wall.

"Dr Coal?" I asked him, I remember sitting on the edge of my bed, wrapped in my white sheets. I knew something was wrong, but Coal would never tell me anything about his life outside these white walls. "Are you okay?" I asked again, hoping he would stop pacing around—I was becoming dizzy.

"My apologies, Noah, I have a tight schedule today, so my visit will be short," Coal finally replied, scraping his hand through his hair.

"Aren't they always?" I asked him, confused and worried that something had happened to him. He wasn't the calm and collected spirit I knew from the day I woke up.

"Noah, how are you feeling today? Have you been eating plenty of fruit like I suggested?" he asked, ignoring my question. He reached into his briefcase and handed me an apple, just like the day before.

"Can I be honest with you?" I asked him, taking the apple from his hand. He looked at me for a second, nodded and sat beside me on the edge of my bed. "I'm ready to go outside again, I want to contact my family. I know you said you would help me, but I still haven't heard from them and this is the fifth day now," I told him, hoping he'd give me good news. I had hoped he'd surprise me in that moment, tell me they were on their way.

"Noah, we've been through this. I want you to get back on your own two feet again, but it's just too dangerous for you out there. Your health is important, and my only goal is to help you recover again," he told me as he placed his hand on my shoulder. "We don't want you to have a relapse, and just think, you get to stay at home and relax," he continued. "Trust me, your family have been informed and they want to leave you to rest for a few more days before they visit. Trust me, Noah, everything will be okay in time," he smiled and squeezed my shoulder.

Looking back to this moment, I wish I had the courage to do more for myself and take the risk of leaving sooner. I was so absorbed in my own mind, that I'd forgotten about my life outside of these white walls.

"It's very important that you eat, Noah," Coal said, encouraging me to eat the apple. "Otherwise, we'll have to try a different method," he told me, I could tell he was still frustrated about something.

"Such as?" I asked, worried about his next answer.

"There are other treatments available if you don't eat, but they will be uncomfortable for you. Trust me, Noah, it's better if you eat the fruit," he told me, before finding his feet again. "Before I go, have you had anymore dreams?" he asked. I was waiting for that question from the minute he walked through the door. I wondered what a man like Coal would want with someone else's dreams? He always seemed more interested than concerned, and that frightened me a little. I could never understand what my dreams had to do with my recovery or my family, and even on the fifth day I didn't want to share them with him.

"No!" I lied, again. "If I remember anything, I'll write it down," I told Coal, hoping that he'd buy my lies for another day and that his short visit was over.

"Please do, I'll stop by again—soon," he told me. I was so distracted that I never heard him leave. I was so consumed by a different presence on the other side of my window. Without hesitation, I walked towards the window and placed my hand on the glass. There she was, standing by the tall tree, wearing the same white dress as the day before—Aurora.

Chapter Eight
Numbers

THE only way we would listen was to rid us of all the distractions; the ones that made our brains numb, blind to the truth and deaf to the voices from within. We were asleep, but completely awake in our dreams. When we finally opened our eyes, we saw reality; nothing was what it seemed, apart from one thing—the connection we all shared.

When the universe gives us a door, we should open it—I did. I opened the glass window to join Aurora by the tall tree. She was standing there, facing down at the two broken branches, apologising to the tree as if it were listening.

"Sorry for what?" I asked her as I approached. I noticed she was hiding her hands against the fabric of her dress and her face wet; I could almost taste the salt from her tears.

"I'm frightened!" she told me. I could sense the fear in her voice, and I remembered how scared I was the first few days after the accident.

"You have nothing to be frightened of," I tried to convince her. That was when I realised, she had also suffered something terrible. Even in those moments of not knowing who I really was, I had to be brave for her—she was only a child. "Do you live with your parents here?" I asked her, noticing that she was always by herself in the garden. She shook her head and frowned; still standing, staring at the broken branches below her.

"I keep having the same dreams," Aurora finally told me. When she finally turned towards me, I could see that those big blue oceans were polluted with fear—that angered me.

"Do you want to talk about it?" I asked her, hoping that she would find trust in me, even though I was a stranger to her.

"There was a man counting in a different language…" she stopped and apologised to me. Even her dreams sounded familiar, like we shared them as well. "Numbers!" she continued, shaking her head in confusion.

"Numbers?" I asked, I felt my heart beating faster as I remembered my own dream with the Eskimo; he was mumbling something to me, something I couldn't understand. Aurora looked at me, she could tell I was in deep thought. "What did he look like?" I asked, waiting for her to describe the same dream.

"I'm sorry," she said as she ran off back towards her window.

I ran after her, begging her to come back, "Aurora, wait, come back!" I shouted, but she closed her window behind her.

"You don't get much out of that one!" a voice called out from the next window. As I turned, I saw a strange lady walking towards me. As she came closer, I noticed she was a lot older than me; mid-forties with short, curly hair and she had a great smile.

"Violet!" she smiled, giving me her hand to shake. Her fingers were thin and wrinkly, but I could tell by the handshake that she was tougher than she looked.

"Noah!" I replied, smiling back at her. "You know her?" I asked Violet about Aurora, hoping she could tell me more than I already knew. Violet was the type of woman who'd help you with anything in life if she saw you struggling. She had a kindness in her warm green eyes, and wrinkles made from wisdom.

"I know that she's just as lost as the rest of us here!" Violet told me, as she looked towards Aurora's window. "It must be harder for a girl her age though," she continued, "waking up in a strange place, surrounded by strange faces…" I could see Violet's mind beginning to wonder in that moment, looking just as lost as we were.

"Wait, so she doesn't have family here?" I asked her, I was becoming concerned. Even then, I was naïve; deaf to every word that Violet spoke that day. I wish I'd listened to her words more carefully; I wish I was present.

Violet let out a short nervous laugh and looked at me with her earthy green eyes. Her expression changed, and she became more serious. "Look around you, honey! None of us have family here!" she said in calm voice, patting my shoulder, before walking off in the opposite direction again.

I should've known in that moment that something was off. I was left standing there, lost for words. I wondered how she would have known that I hadn't seen my family for days.

As Violet walked off, she raised her hands in the air. That was the moment I realised that the strange naked lady from the previous night, was her.

Chapter Nine
The Watering Can

VIOLET wasn't the only strange creature that lurked around those gardens, there were others as well. Others I was yet to meet. I looked back across to Aurora's window, hoping that she'd be okay, and whoever was inside there with her would keep her safe. Without consciously knowing, I was feeding into the same fear she was, and that's exactly what they wanted.

When I made my way back towards the tall tree, I noticed where the branches had broken off. I could tell then, that the tree was ancient; even older than the tree from my childhood memory. It grew from the centre of the garden, reaching around 100 feet in height. The two branches had broken from a thicker branch; approximately two branches above my paper snowflake. On the fifth day, the broken branches would remain a mystery.

From the right-hand side of the garden I noticed a man walking around the outside of the white buildings with a silver watering can. He was an elderly black man, dressed in white overalls and wearing a straw sun hat. He was whistling away, minding his own business. I'd never seen him around before that day, I presumed he was just the gardener. I know now that nobody was what they appeared to be; everyone here had depths that most would drown in.

As I focused my attention back towards the tree, I noticed that same butterfly from the first days. I remembered it because of the unique pattern in its wings. After flying around in front of me, I watched it land on my paper snowflake, hanging a few branches above. As the butterfly landed, I replayed the memory from the orphanage over in my head. The butterfly came flying towards me again then landed onto the second broken branch below me. The signs were everywhere, I just had to open myself to them.

On the fifth day, I regained another important memory as I touched the second broken branch that lay beneath the tall tree.

ZWEI

At first, I was surrounded by laughter; the sound of children playing around me, but I couldn't see in the beginning. There was just a white emptiness, and the laughter turned into gentle whispers. I could feel the heat from the sun; heating my body as the whispers become clearer.

"We must hurry, Noah!" The same voice as my first memory speaks to me—that sweet voice. My vision becomes clearer and I was back in my six-year-old body. I was sitting on the branch of a familiar tree, that same tree from before. There was nobody else there with me, just the voice of a girl, someone familiar.

"Where are you?" I asked her, looking around the other branches of the tree.

"I'm right here, silly!" The voice replies, laughing, but there was still no one in sight. I realised the sound was coming from the inside of my hands that were cupped together. I could see a white light escaping from the gaps of my fingers. I opened my hands slowly to reveal this beautiful white rose. The rose continued to speak to me; every word filling me with its light. The petals sparkled in the sunlight, and I could feel my heart beat faster as the girl counted to ten.

"We need ten guardians, each will symbolise the ten trees that circle this land," the rose continued. "They will keep us safe!"

I realised the tree I was sitting on was one of the ten that formed a perfect circle. "Together, we will create one guardian every day until we have ten," the rose told me. I noticed the empty space in the middle of the circle, I recognised the land. The rose counted again, "One, two, three, four, five, six, seven, eight, nine…"

"Ten?" I heard a man's voice from behind as I came back into the present moment. I turned to be greeted by the elderly

36

black man who was standing there with his watering can. He wasn't much shorter than me, and had a grey stubble growing from his chin. "You looked like you were in your own little world there. I didn't want to disturb you, but I think you might have dropped this!" he said as he handed me a silver locket. I noticed it was the same locket Aurora was wearing when I first met her.

"Oh, thanks…" I replied, hoping the man would give me his name as he placed the locket into my hands.

The man took off his straw sun hat with one hand, "Rudo!" he introduced himself as he gave me a nod. "Please to meet you," he said, giving me his hand.

"Noah!" I replied, shaking his hand. He smiled and repeated my name back to me.

"I recognise your face…" Rudo said, in deep thought.

"You do? I don't remember, sorry," I told him, trying to remember if I'd met him before the accident.

"Hmm… Maybe It'll come back to me, Noah, I can barely remember yesterday!" he laughed, placing his sun hat back onto his head.

That was when I began to realise that everyone I'd met over the past few days had trouble remembering anything.

"Rudo?" I asked him. He looked at me and smiled, I could see it in his dark brown eyes; the same confusion that filled the eyes of everyone that day.

"Yes?" Rudo replied, I could see he was masking his sadness with humour.

"Where is your family?" I asked, I was beginning to realise why everyone here was feeling alone.

"I… I don't remember," he replied, his expression turned blank as he dropped the watering can by his side.

My heart started racing as I replayed the last few days over in my mind. I was beginning to see a pattern in everyone's behaviour; none of us could remember anything. I realised that everyone I'd met, including myself, was wearing white. We were all surrounded by the same building that reached over thirty feet in height. None of us could remember our pasts, our families and the conversation with Violet earlier began to sink in. And during that day, I realised; that place wasn't our home—it was a prison.

Chapter Ten
The Sleepers

THE realisation of my reality crippled me inside; that moment I found it hard to breathe, and my legs became weak. I wanted Rudo to reassure me, tell me that he had remembered where his family was and that it was just his age catching up with him. His face remained frozen and I was beginning to see double. I struggled to speak to him, and even if I could—he was completely lost in his own mind.

Have you ever had one of those dreams where you're being chased by something or someone? One of those dreams that require you to run but your physical body becomes detached and running seems impossible; your actions become slower and whatever was chasing you, caught you before you even considered running. That's how I felt in that moment, the moment I tried to run back towards Aurora's window. My legs almost gave up as I approached the window, and the sound of my voice was overpowered by the loud pounding in my heart as I shouted, "Aurora!"

When I finally reached Aurora's window, I placed my shaking hands upon the glass. "Aurora, I need to talk with you, please!" I shouted, trying to see through its thick tinted layers. I curled my hands into hammers; banging them against the window in hope she would open it. The sound echoed through the garden, attracting Violet's attention. I could see her from the corner of my eye, walking towards me, trying to understand the situation.

"Noah! Stop!" I heard Violet shout towards me, almost through her teeth. "If they see you, they'll reset the circle!" The words spoken by Violet confirmed everything—she knew more than the rest of us.

"Who's they?" I asked Violet as she approached with her hands up, almost as if she were trying to capture the noise I was creating. Before she could continue, I noticed an opening halfway up the wall that surrounded us. A large black square appeared as the white bricks shifted, allowing another device to emerge.

An unfamiliar voice projected from the device, "All sleep systems activated!" I realised that was what Aurora was trying to tell me when she mentioned the sleepers!

I looked over at Rudo, who was also now focused on the device, he was even more confused. Part of me felt this overwhelming urge to walk over and comfort him. Violet tried to cover her ears when the device started counting backwards from six, but the sound that followed when the device finished would penetrate through the gaps of her fingers.

The sound echoed throughout the garden, so loud that even the birds on the treetops started dropping—a lucky few, fled into the sky above. The high-pitched tone was unbearable; I felt a warm liquid trickle down my neck, and when I wiped my neck, I saw blood. Just like the birds, we dropped too—one by one.

Chapter Eleven
Outsider

II

"HE'S AWAKE!" I heard the familiar voice of a girl shout in the distance. When I finally came to my senses I realised that the voice was Uki. I could feel the cold air circulating around the inside of my ears, my nose, like a thermometer; determining the freezing temperatures. I could finally move my arms, and my fingers became animated. I put my fingers into my ears to check for blood—there was no trace of it.

"Noah?" I heard Aput rushing over to me, the sound of his feet crunching through the snow that lay beneath me. I was wrapped in layers of fur that protected me from the icy environment. "Let me help you!" Aput insisted, pulling my upper body gently off the ground. His hands were warm, heated from the fire inside the igloo. "Easy..." Aput grabbed onto my shoulders to steady my uneasy body.

Living between two strange realities, with no conscious memory of the past, was unsettling. I struggled to comprehend which was real; the physical and emotional elements in both made it hard to determine. "How long was I out?" I asked Aput, hoping my reality would play out until, eventually, making sense of which was real. I felt safe there, no longer confined by large prison walls.

"A few hours or so..." Aput replied, handing me a set of fur gloves. "Here, these will keep you warm," he continued, assisting me with them. Aput could tell I was curious about the fur as I examined the brown strands of hair, trying to reconstruct them in my mind. "Caribou!" He told me, it was as if he knew the question I was afraid to ask.

"Caribou?" I asked, embarrassed that I had no idea what he meant. I found safety within his big brown eyes, I knew there was so much goodness inside of him. Wherever I was, I was lucky to be rescued by this tribe.

"Maybe you have come to know them as the reindeer…" he told me, reminding me of the famous winter creature I'd once forgotten. "For centuries our ancestors hunted them, the caribou, an animal that can endure the cold. The only way to survive out here was to become like caribou." He could tell I was afraid of the idea of hunting animals, my eyes widened, ready to remove the fur from my hands.

"Don't worry Noah, this one died from natural causes!" Aput assured me, placing his hands upon mine to stop me from exposing them to the cold. "Our tribe does not hunt land animals, we have a peace treaty with the Borean." I was still unsure about the thought of wearing a dead animal's skin, but I trusted Aput, and became more relaxed.

"Who are they? The Borean?" I asked him, I could see that Ahnah was listening; she was sitting next to the fire, cradling Uki. My question grabbed her attention, and Aput turned towards her. Ahnah looked at him, shaking her head in disapproval. Aput turned his attention back towards me and smiled.

Aput looked into my eyes and replied, "That's a great question Noah, nobody has ever really met one…except…" Before he could finish, he was interrupted by the sound of Ahnah who smacked the snow towards him with her hands.

I looked at Ahnah, desperate to know the rest of Aput's story, "Except who? I want to know," I asked.

"It is also in our treaty that we don't discuss the treaty with outsiders!" Ahnah replied, still focused on Aput. Ahnah was only trying to protect her family, she was definitely the brains of the tribe, Aput was the protector, and Uki…like myself, she was still a mystery—yet to be solved.

Ahnah was right, I was indeed an outsider, but even in this winter wonderland I felt safer than I ever before. I picked up the courage and pulled myself off the ground. My face became warmer, the closer I approached the burning fire where I joined both Ahnah and Uki.

I gazed into Ahnah's eyes through the crackling sparks from the fire, and asked her, "Aput told me his name means snow, what does yours mean?" I could feel Aput's eyes watching us from behind.

"Here, it means a wise woman!" she told me. I could tell that deep down Ahnah was afraid of something. I could hear the nervousness in her tone, "Why do you ask?" she asked, glancing over at Aput, who shortly joined us by the fire.

"Because, right now…I could use some of your wisdom, Ahnah. You and your family found me and saved me from the cold, I want to thank you for that. I think you found me for a reason, I'm not sure what that is yet, but any information you can give me would be a lot of help right now," I replied, hoping that she felt my sincerity.

Ahnah told Uki to fetch my backpack once again, and took a deep breath before replying. "Aput, and the others found you buried in the snow, you were lucky. They thought you were dead! There was no sign of anyone else, just you and your backpack." Uki finally handed me my backpack, I didn't recognise it. It was a black nylon zipper, and when Uki placed it in my hands, it felt almost empty. "You really don't remember how you got here?" Ahnah asked as I pulled the zip to open it up.

"No, are you sure this was all I had?" I asked, apprehensive at first to look inside.

"Yes, my men searched the area, but this was all they could find!" Aput replied. The first thing I pulled out was a silver compass, followed by a map. After I pulled out the map, I reached into the bottom of the backpack to search for anything else. The last remaining item was something I'd seen from my past memories, except it was dead—a white rose.

Chapter Twelve
An Impossible Journey

THERE they were again; those sweet memories of holding the white rose came rushing back to me. I began to question myself; was this the same rose from my memories? If so, what happened to the brilliant white light? What happened to that angelic voice that spoke those sacred verses from the bible? I was becoming lost in my own mind again, trying to figure everything out.

"Noah?" Aput called my name, he could tell I was distracted—lost again. "Don't worry my friend, we will help you find your way again." I looked over at him, his eyes looked so promising, and I had to have trust in him—I didn't have any other choice out there. I placed the dead flower back inside my backpack and opened the map up. The map was of the Antarctic region, I had previously marked my direction and crossed off my destinations. There was one circle left on that map—the North Pole. Aput leaned in closer to get a look at my map, "Can I see this?" he asked me.

I looked at his curious face, without hesitation, I handed him the map. "Sure," I replied, after handing over the map, his expression changed from curious to concerned. Aput showed Ahnah the map, then they both looked up at me. "What's wrong?" I asked, confused about the map, confused about everything.

"Impossible…" Ahnah looked at Aput, still holding onto Uki, who looked just as confused as me. "We can't help you Noah, it's too dangerous!" she told me, shaking her head. I still had no idea why I was trying to reach that location in the first place.

"Noah, this is the land of the Borean, no tribe has ever tried to cross their territory. You seek the impossible, the journey alone is a suicide mission!" Aput told me, as he handed the map back to me.

I was still completely lost in my own mind, the fact that I couldn't remember anything frustrated me. I knew I was there for a reason, I was living between two very real realities, and I needed all the answers I could find, even if that meant stepping into unknown territory. Giving up wasn't an option, and if I had to complete my journey with no memory and no help, then so be it.

"I am very grateful for all you have done for me, I still can't remember how I got here but I believe that's where I'll find my answers. I will continue my journey by myself, even if it seems impossible!" I told them, even though I dreaded the idea of wondering those frozen lands by myself. "I just need to ask one last thing. It might be a great help to me…" I said, clasping my hands together, hoping they would give me one last piece of information.

"Yes?" Aput replied. I could tell he felt guilty about the whole situation, there was this look in his eyes, after all, he was the alpha.

"You told me that, nobody has ever met the Borean, except one. Maybe this person can help me, can you at least tell me where I could find them?" I asked, hoping that they would guide me in the right direction. Aput looked at Ahnah who nodded, agreeing to give me this last piece of important information, even if it meant putting their tribe in danger. I think the thought of me leaving the tribe in peace comforted Ahnah. I didn't blame her, she was only trying to protect her people—after all I was a complete stranger to them.

"Inuksuk is his name. He is angakkuq, he is our spirit healer, the shaman amongst our people," Aput told me. "My tribe will take you to him in the morning…" Aput's voice began to fade, I could see his mouth moving but there was no sound.

I stood up and shut my eyes; trying to focus my senses again, but closing them made me feel more unstable. "Noah?" I heard Ahnah's voice fade in and out, before dropping to the ground. I could feel Aput's hands around me, trying to help me back off the ground but I was losing consciousness again.

There I was again, falling back into the blackness, the only sound I could hear was that same familiar voice of the rose. The girl's voice started counting slowly, "One, two, three, four, five, six, seven, eight, nine…" before she could finish, I felt my body temperature rise as I woke up. There I was, again, surrounded by those white walls that imprisoned me. A familiar face came into focus as I regained consciousness, and the fear that I had left behind filled me to the core.

"Noah? Are you awake?" a familiar man's voice asked, and then I realised it was him—Coal.

Chapter Thirteen
The Circle of Consciousness

I wasn't sure how long I'd been asleep, or how I got back into my room. The last thing I remembered was falling to the ground after realising this place was… "Noah?" Coal repeated my name several times, interrupting my thought process.

"Where am I?" I asked him, I didn't want to hear the answer; I didn't want to listen to anymore lies from him. "Don't lie to me, I know this isn't my home, these people aren't…" before I could finish, Coal interrupted, handing me a glass of water.

"Let's go over this slowly, Noah. I know you must be feeling very confused!" He told me, creating a small space on my bed so he could sit beside me. "Please…drink up, you should keep yourself hydrated."

"Please tell me where I am?" I asked, looking over to the window. I wasn't sure if it was the same day, or if I'd slept through an entire day again. I quickly glanced over to the main door in the room, then up at the strange device that was attached to the ceiling. "That thing up there, I remember trying to leave…"

"Noah, please, let me explain everything." Coal interrupted, trying to keep me in a calm state of mind, but the fear was taking over, the only thing I wanted to do was escape. I looked into the glass of water once again, then back at the door. My hands became colder the tighter I gripped onto the glass, and my flight mode kicked in. Suddenly, I threw the glass of water over his face, into his eyes; I needed a few moments ahead of him to escape. Before he could react, I was already off the bed and on my way to the main door.

My heart was pounding. I didn't look back at him once, the only thing I wanted was to get out of that place as fast as I could. I felt the adrenaline firing through my body as I approached the door. Before I could even touch the handle, I'd triggered the device above my bed. That moment confirmed that I was indeed a prisoner, and I wasn't getting out so easy. The door was locked, and the device suddenly stopped.

"I'm not your enemy Noah, I don't want to hurt you, but if you don't cooperate…" I heard Coal behind me, the sound of his footsteps approaching closer. I turned around to see him drying his face with a small black remote in his hands, a remote that seemed to control the device—the sleeper.

"You've been lying to me all along, and the others! What is this place?" I shouted at him, looking around for any other possible exits—there were none. I could feel my hands shaking, the rush of adrenaline was taking over completely, and I was finding it hard to breathe.

"Please, take a seat Noah, you're in shock I understand," he said to me, pointing towards the bed, but that was the last thing I wanted to do. I looked over to the window, I thought about the others: Aurora, Violet, Rudo… I wondered if they were okay, if they knew what was happening in that moment. Nothing was making any sense, I was ready to run towards the window. Coal could see in my eyes that I was ready to make another run for it, cause some kind of commotion. Before I could run, the main door behind me opened and two other people entered, immediately grabbing a hold of my arms.

"Who are you people? What do you want with me?" I yelled, trying to fight them off, but they were stronger than me, two other men, both wearing white.

"Thank you!" Coal thanked the two men who forced me into the white armchair by the bed. They tied my hands to the arms of the chair, and my feet to the legs so I couldn't run. I shouted for help several times, but then realised that I was surrounded by large white walls out there, and wherever I was, help would be the last thing I would attract. Coal dismissed the two men then crouched in front of me.

"Do you feel calm enough to listen to me yet?" Coal asked. I was beginning to understand the blackness in those eyes of his,

47

I was beginning to understand that he didn't possess any empathy.

"Are you even a doctor?" I asked. I had so many unanswered questions circling in my mind. Coal patted my shoulder and grinned, I wish I could have wiped that stupid grin off his face. The only thing I felt towards him was anger. He was never who he said he was in the beginning, and any trust I had for him was gone.

"I prefer scientist, but I'm not the important one here Noah, you are!" he told me, getting back onto his feet again. "Well, you and the others…" he continued, glancing over at the window. "I see you've already been acquainted. You are all very special individuals; each possessing a unique gift, that is why we chose you," he said, pacing around the room.

"Chose us? For what?" I asked, still angry with him, unable to move my body.

"The future of humanity, Noah!" he told me, walking towards me slowly. "You'll come to understand that the others here are just like you, in their own ways. You all have a gift…" he said, looking deeper into my eyes. "We created this place especially for you, a place where you would be unaffected by the outside world; the distractions, corruption, disease, the wars. Each of you have the gift of empathy. You all possess a specific type, something that humanity lost a long time ago."

Coal crouched down beside me again, "This place wasn't built to make you a prisoner, it was built to keep you safe from that world. You and the others are the last remaining hope, we chose you for a reason," he said in a clam tone, but I was still finding it hard to follow—I still felt trapped. Coal untied my arms and legs, "My apologies Noah, this was the only way to get you to listen to me without you trying to run away. I hope we can start over and start rebuilding the future, once and for all," he told me, freeing my hands slowly.

"I still don't understand? Where are we? Why can't I remember anything?" I asked him, desperate to know everything, desperate to remember who I really was. Coal turned and walked towards the garden window.

"They say that to solve a problem, we must go straight to the root of that problem, right? Well we did, we came to the place that needed our help most. This place is home to many endangered species. Poverty, disease, war…Africa. Did you know, that it's also home to one of the oldest plant species in the world?" Coal pointed towards the tall tree in the garden, "The great baobab tree, amongst many others. We discovered that this tree is over ten thousand years old, making it the oldest tree in Africa. Some believe that this was the original tree of life, so we built this place around it. The *Circle of Consciousness.*" Coal smiled as he admired the tall tree in the garden, I could see he was proud of his accomplishments, but I was still confused, and angry.

"How does any of this explain why I'm here or help me remember who I am?" I asked him, I was becoming more annoyed.

"We know that humans have a consciousness, but we also discovered that plants have a consciousness as well. Plants are the oldest living beings on this earth. Despite all the events that have occurred on Earth, they continue to grow, adapt and communicate with each other. We destroy them, and yet they still forgive us, provide for us. Without them we wouldn't have survived this long. They give us the nutrients we need to survive. We're only now discovering all these cures for the diseases that plague this world," Coal told me, still focused on the garden.

Coal was right about that, I couldn't deny the connection I had with nature, and I saw it in the others too. Even though I was still angry, another outburst wouldn't help me in any way, the only thing I could do in that moment was listen, try to understand.

"Our mission here is to find the connection between human consciousness, and plant consciousness. That's why we selected you. You have a strong connection with nature, you understand it, and it, understands you," he said. Coal turned to look at me, he was right about that too, the trees from my childhood memory, the rose. I was connected somehow, but I wondered how he could possibly know? What else happened during my life that I couldn't remember, how did I get to that point?

"Not only that, Noah, you are an intuitive empath, you can feel people's emotions on a deeper level, you can feel the energy of others around you. Your dreams…you can receive information telepathically through dreaming. They say that plants speak to us when we're asleep, when the world is quiet and we're less distracted by the world around us. Most people can't switch off from the world around them, that's why it was important to erase your memory—the others' memories too," he said. Coal stopped for a moment, and looked back out the window towards the tall tree. I was lost for words, I struggled to comprehend everything he was telling me. When did the world become so dark?

I realised why Coal had been so interested in my dreams from the beginning, but I couldn't move my mouth to get any confirmation from him. I wondered if the rest of the world knew about this place. Did I agree to this? Did I have a choice? What about the others? Aurora? My head felt as though it was about to explode. If Coal was right about me being so empathic, why couldn't I find any emotion in him?

"I know, right now you probably think that what we're doing here is wrong, but you'll come to understand that it's for the greater good. You are our last hope, Noah, if we can communicate with nature, maybe we can find the secret of life, the key to a better future," Coal said as he looked at me again. "It's important that we all help each other here, we only have one rule: don't enter anyone else's room, we respect each other's privacy."

Coal turned and walked towards the main door. I still had so many unanswered questions. "Wait!" I shouted. "Was I really involved in an accident?" I asked, stopping Coal in his tracks, he didn't turn back.

"Erasing someone's memory isn't easy, we figured that if we lied about the cause, pretended this was your home…replaced your old memories with new ones, you wouldn't try to leave so easily. Eventually we were going to tell you the truth, we needed you to become stable first. I suggest you help the others feel more comfortable too without resetting the circle again," he said.

"And, what if I wanted to leave? Do I have a choice?" I asked before he opened the main door. Part of me wanted to follow him, then I realised where I was, even if I escaped this facility, where would I go? I was in Africa.

Before Coal left the room, he sighed, "I'm afraid not!" before closing the door.

Chapter Fourteen
Creature of the Night

COAL gave me the confirmation I needed—like the others, I too was a prisoner. The sun was beginning to set, but my mind was still wide awake. The last thing I wanted to do was sleep. I thought about going outside to find the others, tell them everything I knew, but there was no sight of anyone.

The only thing I could do was use the time I had to cooperate until I found a better way to escape that place. Maybe the world was in complete chaos; maybe Coal was right; maybe we were the last hope for humanity. But we didn't have a choice, they made us forget about our lives, everything we once knew—was gone.

If Coal was right about me and my dreams, maybe I could use them to my advantage, maybe the others could help. I thought about Aurora, she was so young, her life was only beginning. Even if she was gifted, these people shouldn't get to decide her fate.

I kept thinking about the Arctic, another reality that only recently started occurring, as far as I could remember. Maybe that was my escape, maybe something within me already knew and I was already preparing myself. I found it hard to determine what was real. Nothing made sense to me; maybe I could play this reality out too. I thought about the tall tree, my paper origami; I had already been connecting with this tree. I remembered the memories only came back to me whenever I touched the broken branches, maybe the tree was responding to me in some way.

I replayed the previous days over and over, trying to make sense of everything. The more I replayed them, the closer I found myself to the window. Was the tall tree really communicating with me? I realised that the two broken branches were still by the bottom of the tall tree, where I left them before I set the sleepers off. In that moment, I was beginning to discover the pattern, not fully, but I could feel something in the works.

I looked up to see my paper origami still hanging on the branches, still untouched. Every time I added something, I would recover a lost memory. Was it just a coincidence, or was the tree really listening to me? Was it giving me something in return?

I remembered Coal telling me that each of us possessed a different type of empathy. I couldn't help but wonder about the others; Rudo, Violet, Aurora, and what their abilities were. Maybe if I knew more about each of them I could find another way out of that place sooner. The sun had nearly set, and I had work to do.

I tried to remember the details; something to symbolise the last dream about the Arctic, something from my backpack that I could recreate. The sheets of paper where still scattered underneath the bed, along with the roll of string and other craft materials that I never found useful. My dreams where important to Coal, whether I wrote about them, or recreated them somehow using my imagination. My dreams where the only thing Coal couldn't destroy. He needed them, which meant I could continue my own mission without him interfering.

I struggled with the third recreation. I kept hearing the voice of the girl in my head with every fold. The third piece was something special; it triggered something inside me, bringing tears to my eyes. "We will get through this Noah," I whispered to myself. After the last fold, I held it against the window to appreciate its beauty in the light of the dying sun. There it was, another paper masterpiece—the white rose.

The sun had almost completely fallen into the horizon for another day, and I ran to the tall tree to add my third piece. I was so busy concentrating on reaching the tree, I didn't notice someone else running from a different direction in the garden, so fast—we crashed into each other, and fell to the ground.

"Duìbuqǐ!" I heard a female voice shout. As I lifted myself off the ground I realised it was another prisoner there, an Asian female, not much older than myself.

"Are you okay?" I asked, helping her off the ground. She had short black hair, only a few inches shorter than me and she was picking up different leaves that she dropped. "Sorry, I didn't see you there!" I apologised. I realised she had her own little mission, maybe we all did. I wanted to ask her questions, but she didn't speak any English. I apologised again, and she ran off again into the garden. I hoped I hadn't hurt her in anyway. I hoped she realised I was on her side, if she even knew there was a side.

There were six windows in that garden, which meant there was another prisoner I had yet to meet. In that moment, I picked up my paper rose and continued towards the tall baobab tree. I noticed that all the birds that dropped from the tree earlier that day had disappeared, I wondered if they had survived or if someone had taken them away. I decided to gather the pile of broken branches and hide them on the other side of the tree where it was more secluded. If this tree was really responding to me, I didn't want Coal to know. I didn't want him to interfere.

I made my way up the tree, and sat for a moment before threading the rose. I remembered the dead white rose from my backpack, I wondered why I had been carrying it, where was I taking it to? I tied the rose to the branch above me, beside the snowflake, this tree was becoming my diary of dreams.

Darkness had finally painted the sky black, but the night was so clear, and the stars sprayed across the cosmos like a bright splash of glitter. If I didn't appreciate the stars before, I did then, I was envious that even in darkness they were still shining—I was yet to find my light.

My wondering mind almost lifted me into the atmosphere before I heard a loud growl. My heart started beating faster than normal. I could feel something wasn't right. I looked around, still holding onto the branches of the tree, I could feel my grip becoming tighter. I remembered where I was, and the animals that could be lurking outside of those walls. Land animals would find it difficult to even attempt the climb over those large white walls. Before I could ease my mind, I heard another growl, followed by the sound of leaves rustling in the garden below me.

I could feel the bark of the tree cutting into my skin as I gripped onto it even harder, and from the shadowy plants emerged moving black circles—a black panther.

Chapter Fifteen
The Night I *Died*

"HELP!" I shouted. I could feel the bark from the baobab breaking underneath my palms as I try to ease my balance whilst the adrenaline took over my body. The panther growled even louder but couldn't see me. I realised, however, that it was only a matter of time. Shouting for help would only make the situation worse. I had to be smart, and stay calm if I was going to survive.

The panther was looking around the garden below, it knew there was someone else out there. I knew that I could only climb so far up the tree, and if the hungry predator could climb, I had no chance. I looked around the garden, hoping to see the Asian girl but she was gone. I wondered if the beast had already harmed her, or if she'd returned to her room. There was no sign of any-one, all six windows were closed, except one—mine.

I remembered the sleepers; how I triggered them all at once when I tried to enter Aurora's room. Maybe I could convince the panther to enter mine. So I reached onto the branch above me, and silently moved along to the nearest set of twigs. The adren-aline was making it hard to breathe properly, my heartbeat was becoming louder by each step, since I was terrified to fall from the tree. Eventually, I made it to the first set of smaller branches, took a deep breath, and snapped one off.

The panther was becoming more suspicious, more aware of my presence there after breaking of that branch. I tried to steady my breathing and slowly shuffled back to the trunk of the tree. After steadying my balance again, I aimed for my window, and launched the branch into the direction of my window. The branch spiralled in the air, then dropped, just metres in front of the panther. It wasn't enough to set off the sleepers, and the panther didn't even budge.

I knew I had to try again. I had no other option, so I grabbed onto the branch above me again, but before I could shuffle back towards the branch, I slipped on the thicker branch below me. I yelled as I hit the branch below, grabbing it with both hands as I slid off to the side. I couldn't see, but I could feel the panther watching me as it approached the tree. "Help!" I screamed even louder, hoping that someone would hear me.

The panther let out a loud roar and I heard its claws sink into the bark as it made its way up the tree. I was losing all hope. There was no way I could survive this, and the adrenaline was making it hard to hold on any longer. I was dangling below the branch with no body strength to pull myself back up. From the corner of my eyes, I met the panther's as it climbed onto the same branch. "Please, someone, anyone..." I whispered to myself, praying that someone would help me in time. I didn't want to die like that. I didn't want to leave the world as a prisoner with no conscious memory of the past. I could feel the panther's claws scratching against the branch as it moved towards me in a stealthy manner.

I took one more deep breath before closing my eyes, then I decided it was time to let fight mode take over for once—I let go of the branch and plunged into the grass below. Time was never on my side in that circle, especially there, in that moment.

I winded myself as I hit the ground below and lost my focus for a moment. I could see the light from my bedroom window, and picked myself off the ground. The panther jumped the moment I started running. I could hear its weight as it landed into the grass behind me. I knew the panther would outrun me, but I would keep running regardless.

I heard the panther leap towards me, the sound of its paws leaving the soil as it struck behind me. I nearly made it to my window before closing my eyes and falling onto the grass. The soil was cold as the night cooled the earth, and time felt like it had stopped. They say that when you finally die, its over in an instant, like a flash in time, and then you're gone. My death felt like an eternity that night, I almost never lifted my head from the soil again until I heard the sound of my heart beat, echoing through the ground below me.

The light from my window created a rectangular pool of light against the grass in front of me, there was no sound. Everything was silent. After I lifted myself off the ground, I hesitated to look back. The fifth night, I witnessed something I'll never forget, a wild predator bowing to the hands of another human—Aurora.

Chapter Sixteen
Balance

AURORA was the bravest child I'd ever met. She'd saved my life in that dark moment, and nothing I could do would ever be enough to repay her. She was standing under the starry sky with her back towards me, lit by the light from my window. Her right hand was in front of the panther's face, and the panther bowed its head like it knew her. She was like jungle royalty; ruler of the animal kingdom. That was the first time I'd witnessed her true power, she was an animal empath.

"Don't be afraid Noah, she is our friend," Aurora whispered in a calm voice as I walked towards her slowly. The panther had bright yellow eyes, so powerful, I was intimidated at first glance. Aurora knelt beside the panther, and slowly put her hands against its face. I couldn't believe my eyes at first, I was completely lost for words.

"See, she's beautiful," she whispered again, running her hands through its black spotted fur. Aurora was pure; white like a flash of lightning, watching her connect with the black predator was like watching light and dark meet for the first time. There was balance; like yin and yang—a powerful cosmic duality.

"She…tried to kill me!" I replied, still feeling anxious. Aurora soon made me understand, that so many animals have been misunderstood and given a bad name by the human race for too long. She opened my eyes and asked me to let go of my fear for the creature.

"Come closer, Noah! You need to see her for what she really is," Aurora whispered, taking my hand, and placing it onto the panther's face. Aurora looked at me, "A soul," she said, smiling with her bright blue eyes. The wild cat remained calm, and the fear I once had for this creature was gone. Aurora was right, this animal was just finding its own way in life like the rest of us, another human soul. It had the same right to be here, just like every other human being on the planet.

Aurora closed her eyes then placed her hand upon mine, she awakened me; I witnessed flashes of the panther's life from birth until that moment. I saw all the suffering this creature had been through in life, and why it had become so agitated. The panther's mother was shot by hunters at birth, leaving her to fend for herself as a cub. I could feel the emotion connection between this panther and its mother, a powerful unbreakable bond. I saw the panther being captured, which brought it to this moment. The panther thought I was also an enemy—attacking me made sense, I just didn't understand it before.

The panther's memories still play over in my mind to this day, and whenever I look at an animal, I see that it too has its own place in the world. The panther looked into my eyes. I could feel how distressed this animal had become, and how Aurora made the animal understand that we weren't the real enemy.

"What do we do with her?" I asked Aurora, wondering how the panther got into the gardens in the first place. Before Aurora could reply, the panther instantly fell to the grass, revealing a small syringe pierced into its back. The panther had been shot by a tranquilizer, but there was no one in sight.

"NO!" Aurora shrieked, trying to remove the needle. These people weren't just scientists, they were playing God in the garden of evil. We were just one big test, and there was only one thing we could do—survive.

"Please step away from the animal and return to your rooms immediately!" We heard a voice shout in the distance, but there was no sight of anyone. I could see movement in the distance from behind the plants. Whoever this was wouldn't think twice about putting us to sleep too if we disobeyed. I looked at Aurora who was angry, trying to help the panther.

"Aurora, go. She'll be okay!" I promised her, helping her back onto her feet. We both ran back to our rooms. I remembered the locket that Rudo gave to me, but it was too late, she was gone. When I closed my window, I reached into my pocket to find it; a circular silver locket attached to a long silver chain. A half-moon was engraved onto the surface of the locket, and in the middle of the moon, lay a small quartz crystal.

At first, I didn't want to invade Aurora's privacy by looking into the locket, but I listened to my intuition. Inside the locket was an engraved sun, placed in the very middle, divided into two by the fold. Each half of the inside was filled evenly with the flames of the sun and on the right side was the number ninety, and the left numbered zero. Part of me recognised the numbers, part of me that I had forgotten, part of me that I would eventually remember again. I placed the locket back inside my pocket, hoping to give it back to Aurora the next time we crossed paths.

I paced around the room, still shaken up, checking outside the window to see if the panther had been removed from the garden. Suddenly, all the lights switched off, leaving me in complete darkness. The only thing I could think of, in that moment, was to crawl onto the floor and find my way back to my bed. I couldn't sleep on the fifth night, I lost trust in my surroundings after what happened to me.

Hours later, I heard another thud in the garden, and when daylight finally arrived again, I walked back towards the window. There was no sign of the panther, but the question still remained fresh in my mind; how did it get inside? Was there another way out through the garden? I opened the window and stepped outside, there was no trace of anyone. Where had they gone?

The sun hadn't risen yet, and I could feel the cool soil beneath my feet. I couldn't remember the last time I'd wore a pair of shoes. I circled the garden in search for any other possible entrances—I found nothing. I crouched around the trees in the garden, feeling the ground to make sure the area was completely covered with grass and soil. The feeling of being watched never left—no matter where I was. I finally approached the bottom of the tall tree—where I discovered the third broken branch.

Chapter Seventeen
A Trail of Smoke

O<small>N</small> the sixth day I recovered another valuable memory upon touching the third branch. It was then that I discovered the baobab tree was connecting with me, just like the panther connected with Aurora

DREI

There it was again, that same white rose whispering words into my ear as I wandered deep into the forest. "We need to create ten guardians for each of the ten trees. This place is special Noah, I can feel it!" I find myself in the same centre of the circle of trees, and when I opened my hands, I see the glowing white rose. I fully recognised that forest, I just didn't know how. The rose continued to speak to me, "What creature reminds you of the moon, Noah?" the rose asked.

"A wolf?" I replied, I remembered waking up as a child to the howls of wolves in the mountains. The same mountains that surrounded the forest, which meant this place was close to one thing—my home.

"Exactly! Then we will create ten wolves to protect our circle! Every day from now, we will create a unique wolf— each possessing a different gift!" the rose replied. All I wanted to do was find my way home. It was as if the rose could read my every thought, "You are home, silly! We need to create our first wolf now!"

"How can we create one?" I asked, spinning around to see my surroundings properly. I tried to remember which

parts of the mountains I recognised, my home had to be close by.

"Paper!" the rose whispered slowly, reminding me of the origami I had been creating in the garden, was this how I remembered how to create them in the first place? In the distance I spotted smoke from above the treetops, evaporating into the clear skies above.

"There! I need to go!" I told the rose, leaving the circle and running into the forest to follow the smoke trail.

As I made my way through the forest, the rose started talking in a different language, one I had forgotten, "Uppfuttning, Renhet, Balans, Rytm, Drömmar, Medvetenhet, Visdom, Intuition, Styrka..." before the rose could finish, I'd finally reached my destination. The home I'd grew up in was there, except it was up in flames.

I dropped the broken stick. I could feel my heart beating loud in my chest as I fell to my knees. Was that what really happened? Was I remembering things correctly? If my house really was on fire, was my family there when it happened? All these questions were circling my head, and the more I thought about it, the more enraged I became. I was angry at Coal for wiping my memory, I picked up one of the broken sticks and launched it at the garden walls.

"Why are you doing this to us? I know you're watching! Come out here and face me!" I shouted at the top of my lungs, desperate to attract attention. I walked towards the wall, searching for another opening, another device I could set off.

"Anger won't solve anything Noah!" I heard Violet's voice from behind. I turned to see her standing staring up at the tall tree, she looked so calm. She admired my paper origami before her eyes met mine. "Even if anyone's listening, they don't care about our wants and needs. Trust me, there's no reasoning with these monsters!" She laughed nervously, as she approached closer.

"How can you stay calm? You're a prisoner here too!" I asked in frustration. Violet finally approached, and placed her hand upon my shoulder. I saw sympathy growing within the trees of her bright green eyes—she too could feel my pain.

"Because Noah, if we ever want to get out of this place, we must play them at their own game! We can't be a sore loser if we want to win," she replied, shaking my shoulder as she smiled. Violet was right, we had to be smart if we wanted to escape. "It's only a matter of time before they test us again, we need to be ready for them, we need to come up with a plan!" she told me. Violet was smart, and she knew about the tests, I wondered if she saw what happened the night before.

"I've already looked, I can't find another exit..." I replied, still wondering where the panther made its entrance. "There's no way to climb over the walls..." I continued until Violet covered my mouth.

"We need to be more discreet, if they are really listening the last thing we want is them knowing our plan," she replied, slowly removing her hand from my mouth. "We need to get the others in on this, find a safe place in the garden to meet..." She looked towards the tall tree, placed in the centre of the garden. The baobab was not only my dream diary, but it also became our safe zone—a place we would meet, and devise our plan. "There!" Violet pointed towards the tall tree. "Now we need to find a way to tell the others!"

I remembered the pen I found from the fourth night, the only source of ink we had in the prison. "I know!" I told Violet, before running back to my window to grab some sheets of paper from the pile underneath my bed. We wrote a message on four sheets of paper for the remaining prisoners, a message telling them to meet us at the tall tree come nightfall. We left them upside down, outside of each remaining window. That was the beginning of our escape, all we had to do was wait and hope the others would get the message.

I waited back inside my room by the window, waiting for anyone to appear in the garden. Hours passed and I could feel my eyes becoming heavy. We still had a whole day to wait, and I hoped the others would find their way to the tall tree. I remembered how long it had been since I'd last eaten, my stomach was in pain, and I needed to find a source of energy. The only thing we had were apples, and after two bites, I fell fast asleep in my bed.

My body temperature dropped, I could feel my teeth clattering as the freezing air travelled down my spine. "Noah! Come back!" A familiar deep voice tries to wake me, I could feel their hands shaking my shoulders. As I opened my eyes slowly, I saw a man's face come into focus—it was Aput.

Chapter Eighteen
The Great White Open

III

I believe everything that happens to us in life, happens for a reason. Maybe we don't fully understand what that reason is, but every event leads us to a specific point, and time. When we finally arrive at our final destination, we realise that we are exactly where we should be. Even though I couldn't fully remember who I was before; I was discovering myself all over again. I was given a new identity.

The haunted memories of the past would eventually catch up with me, parts of myself that I hoped wouldn't—parts that I wanted to remain forgotten. "Noah, wake up!" I could hear the voice of Aput, trying to wake me into the world of frozen dreams. I realised we were still in the same place; still protected under the cubes of ice, built by Aput and his tribe.

"How long was I gone this time?" I asked Aput. The fire wasn't as bright and the flames were dying. It seemed brighter; the dark shadows had vanished, and I could see the details of the igloo's structure.

"You slept all night, we need to leave soon if we want to make it to the border by sunset. My family and I will take you there, along with two of my best men who know the northern land well. Are you sure you feel well enough for this journey, Noah?" Aput asked me. Uki was helping Ahnah pack for the trip.

"I'm positive, thank you Aput! I will repay you!" I told him, pulling myself off the ground.

Aput handed me a flask of hot soup, "Drink up, you need all the energy you can get, it's a long journey!" he said. "Once you're finished, I'd like you to meet some of the tribe." The soup was delicious, unlike anything I'd ever tried before. I remembered how little I'd eaten in the prison, and finished every last drop.

Outside the igloo the sun was just rising into the clear blue Arctic sky, and the tribe was larger than I thought. There were exactly twenty other igloos out in the open, isolated by large pine trees, covered in snow. Aput's igloo was the largest amongst the rest, I wondered how long these people had been living here. There were packs of huskies scattered around the tribal village.

"Follow me, Noah!" Aput commanded, as he walked towards two other men, whom I presumed would be joining us on the journey. As we approached, Aput greeted his two tribesmen by placing his nose upon their foreheads, and breathing in. Aput invited me to come closer so he could introduce the two men. "Noah, this is Kallik," pointing towards the tallest man. "Here, Kallik means lightning, you will be sharing his sled," Aput told me, smiling at Kallik.

Even though Kallik was the tallest of the three, he looked as though he was the youngest. "Hi Noah!" Kallik walked towards me, introducing himself, "Do not worry my friend, I won't go too fast for you!" he said, smiling as he patted my shoulder.

"And this one is Toklo!" Aput told me, pointing towards the second man. Toklo was the shortest out the three, and didn't say very much. "He will be taking his own sled, keeping an eye out for any danger, while me and my family take the lead," Aput said.

The thought of danger unsettled me, I knew it was a long journey, but this tribe knew the land and they were my only hope at reaching my destination. After my brief introduction with the tribesmen, we gathered our belongings and set off in our sleds into the open snow. Each sled assisted by the strength of huskies, pulling us through the icy land. Further in the front was Aput and his family, all sharing one sled, then Kallik, and myself behind them. Toklo was the furthest behind, wielding a crossbow with one hand, and holding the ropes of his dogs in the other.

The day was passing quicker than I expected, and we stopped to hydrate ourselves and the dogs. Aput and his family were still in front, he looked behind and waved at us, checking everything was fine. "Where are you heading anyway, my friend?" Kallik asked, handing me a flask of water. I opened my backpack, and pulled out the map.

"I'm trying to get to this place. Aput thinks it's impossible, but I believe this is where I'll find the answers," I told Kallik, handing him the map. He had the same expression as Aput and Ahnah when they first opened the map.

"This is Borean territory!" Kallik told me. I saw the same fear that polluted the eyes of Aput whenever he mentioned them. "Nobody has ever been there, except…"

"Inuksuk?" I interrupted before he could finish.

"Yes, Inuksuk is a very wise shaman. I met him once as a child, but he doesn't take kindly to strangers. I'm surprised Aput is taking you there, you must be important to him," Kallik said, placing my map back into my hands.

"He said he found me in the snow, but I don't have any memory of how I got there!" I replied, trying to remember about my first encounter with Aput and his family. "Can I ask you something, Kallik?" I asked, gazing into his deep brown eyes. He nodded in reply, "What can you tell me about the Borean?" I was becoming curious, I wanted to know exactly what I was headed for.

"I know they made a treaty with my ancestors many years ago. They gave us the land, provided us with food and gave us tools to build our homes. They helped us survive, on three conditions! We would no longer hunt the land animals; we would never cross their border and we would never mention them to outsiders," he whispered, worried that the others would hear. I looked back to see Toklo staring at us, sharpening his arrows.

"Why did Aput tell me anything about them in the first place?" I asked, looking back towards Kallik.

"You already knew about them before he told you…" he replied, pointing to my map.

"They can't be bad if they provided your people with all these things then," I said. I could still see he was worried about discussing them with me, after all I was an outsider.

"They don't anymore!" Kallik looked back at Toklo to make sure he wasn't listening. "Back in 1940, our land was invaded by the outsiders, somehow they found out about the Borean. Hundreds of our people were slaughtered because they wouldn't share any information. It was a dark time. When the Borean saw

66

that we were true to our word, they sent help after the invaders had gone, or so we thought. A few remained under the command of their general, and when the help arrived the family were hunted. Some say that one of them survived, made a lucky escape, but the Borean didn't know our lands like we did. Others say that nobody could survive the cold alone." He looked at me. I was becoming more engrossed in Kallik's story. I wanted to know everything, anything that would help me.

"We were blamed for the slaughter of that family. They thought that we wanted revenge. So, they stopped supplying us with food and tools to build. Luckily, we were able to replicate the tools we had and rebuilt all that was lost. Even to this day, we still never broke our treaty. Our people still don't hunt the land animals, only the creatures of the sea," Kallik told me, I was grateful for his story. Before I could ask anymore, we were interrupted by a loud grunting from the distant pine trees.

"Bear!" Toklo shouted from behind. I could see the immediate fear in Kallik's eyes as he grabbed onto the ropes of the sled.

"We must go, now!" he shouted, placing the ropes into my hands. The grunting was becoming louder, which meant the bear was close. "Hold on, Noah!" he told me, pulling the ends of the ropes. Aput commanded his dogs to run first, then Kallik followed his lead. I could feel my heart beating louder in my chest.

When I turned, I saw a large white polar bear running towards Toklo's sled at full speed. "Help!" Toklo shouted at the top of his lungs, still not moving anywhere. The dogs barked and growled as the bear ran towards them. Toklo aimed his crossbow at the bear who clawed through the ropes that connected the huskies.

"Wait!" I shouted at Kallik, who commanded his dogs to stop. Toklo's dogs broke apart, some running off in fear of the malicious white bear, and others, trying to fight back. An arrow plunged into the bear's leg as Toklo took his first shot. The bear swiped the remaining few huskies with its claws, and continued to run full speed towards Toklo's sled.

"Toklo!" Kallik shouted, jumping out the sled and onto the snow. He ran towards Toklo, but it was too late—Toklo never fired another shot at the bear. Aput stopped further at the front, but even he knew that there was no hope for Toklo. The bear dragged Toklo into the trees by his head; leaving behind a reminder of the dangers that lurked out in the open—a pool of blood.

Chapter Nineteen
The Land of Awareness

EVERYTHING was silent; I could see Kallik screaming at the bear, and the dogs from Toklo's sled, barking and diving back and forth in the snow—but there was no sound. It was as if noise was non-existent during those traumatic moments.

Toklo's blood stained the snow; a gruesome reminder of the reality we were facing. The bear had disappeared, and my sound finally came back, followed by the faint cries of Toklo as he faced his end. Kallik picked up Toklo's crossbow off the ground, and ran back to the sled. I could see Ahnah covering Uki's face in front of us, I hoped she hadn't witnessed the attack. Our sleds took off back into the open.

The remaining hours of that day felt like days. I blamed myself for what happened that day. If it weren't for me, my reckless journey into the unknown, Toklo would still be there. I couldn't even bring myself to apologise to Kallik, knowing he was a close friend from the same tribe. I could tell by his face that he wasn't ready to talk about it.

Kallik was holding the crossbow in his shaking hand, he was also in shock. The sun was finally setting as we approached the entrance to a forest—the tops of the trees were completely covered in sheets of snow. Our sleds came to a stop as we reached the entrance, Aput jumped off his sled and ran towards us. Aput remained calm, this is why he was chosen to be the tribe's leader, but I could tell that deep down he was shaken up.

As Aput approached our sled, he grabbed a hold of Kallik and placed his nose upon his forehead, taking a deep breath before apologising. "He is with the green sky now, my friend." Aput tells Kallik who begins to cry. Aput then turned to me. "Are you okay, Noah?" he asked, placing his hand upon my shoulder. Physically I wasn't hurt, but emotionally, I felt damaged. I couldn't ever remember witnessing anything so brutal before. I was still completely lost for words and nodded in reply.

"We must go by foot from here I'm afraid, it's not much further!" Aput told me, before turning back towards Kallik, "The bear will return once it's had its feast, we must be ready for it!" The rules of hunting land animals didn't apply when it came to self-defence, and I didn't wait for it to come back.

We entered the forest on foot, leaving Kallik behind to guard the dogs. Ahnah was carrying Uki in her arms, just metres in front. I felt safe walking beside Aput who was carrying his own crossbow in his hands, ready for any attack. "I'm sorry about Toklo. This journey wouldn't have happened if I had just listened to you in the first place!" I apologised to Aput.

"This journey wouldn't have happened if I hadn't given my men the order," Aput told me. "My people face great dangers every day Noah, nobody is to blame. Toklo knows the risks of the open snow, the only thing that matters to us is getting you to Inuksuk safely." Aput handed me a flask of water, "Not much further now!" he said, as darkness finally approached.

I could hear the wild animals in the near distance and prayed that the bear was still far away. Darkness had finally taken over, and we stopped in a wide-open space amongst the trees. "Shhh!" Aput silenced our movements. Everything was silent, and we huddled together in the darkness.

The darkness filled up with glowing yellow eyes, we were surrounded by the watchers of the night—a nocturnal audience.

"What are they?" I asked Aput, who was rustling inside of Ahnah's backpack. A bright flame emitted from his hands as he lit his torch. The flames of Aput's torch exposed the lingering creatures that watched us carefully. Aput revealed hundreds of owls perched on the branches of the surrounding trees.

"Look, look!" Uki shouted in amazement, pointing to the owls. Ahnah put her hands around Uki's head and pulled her closer so she could smell her hair. Uki was lucky to have a mother like Ahnah, nothing would ever break their bond.

"We call this the land of awareness!" Aput said as he moved his torch around, revealing more owls. "They are the watchers of the Arctic, the guardians of the shaman, Inuksuk!" He told me as we began to venture further into the woods. "We are safe for now, if danger was close by, the watchers would know!" he said. His words were comforting, and I knew we had to be close.

Further into the trees, we saw a glowing light in the distance. "There!" Aput said, pointing towards what looked like a wreckage. As we got closer, I noticed it was the wreckage of an old plane lit from the inside and converted into a living space. Its wings had been detached, acting as stands that held the wreckage over a man-made cabin. The closer we reached, the lighter my head became.

"Aput! I don't feel okay!" I told him, losing my balance. My vision was becoming blurry and Aput held onto me, passing the torch to Ahnah.

"Almost there, Noah! Stay with us!" he said, lifting me off the ground. He carried me closer to the plane wreckage where I saw the words 'Fokker' written on the body of the plane. The tail was slightly broken but I could make out the number one painted in white. There were two flaming torches by the entrance of the cabin, and as Aput opened the door to the shaman's lair, I could feel my body becoming weaker. "Noah?" I heard Aput, repeating my name, trying to keep me there, but it was too late. I woke up under my white sheets, back behind the same white walls that imprisoned me.

I saw a familiar face drawing towards me, and when I finally became conscious, my heart stopped when I'd finally processed the person staring back at me, "Mother!"

Chapter Twenty
The Plan

FOR a moment I lay wrapped under my white sheets, unable to move. The sight of my mother's face made me remember the apparition from the first days in that place. I reached out to touch her face, she looked exactly the same as how I'd remembered. The memories I had of her where faint; fragments of childhood memories that where almost impossible to hold onto for more than a few seconds. As I reached closer, I saw a circular pool of light reflecting across her face, and the more conscious I became, the more I realised she wasn't really there.

"Good evening, Noah!" Coal's voice filled the quiet room, as he pulled the photo of my mother back towards him. "Took me a while to see the resemblance, but now I see it, you both have the exact same eyes. I bet she also had the potential to change the world, such a waste…" he said, deep in thought. I felt nothing but anger towards Coal. He had taken my life from me and all the memories I ever had of my family.

I clenched my fist and tried to reach towards him, only to realise I was tied to the bed. "Argh!" I clenched my teeth together, "What do you know about my mother?"

Coal leaned in closer, "I know she was also gifted. That's why she was killed," he told me, my heart sunk to the bottom of my chest, and I squeezed my fists even tighter. I could feel the pressure as my arms cut deeper into the straps that held me down when I resisted.

"Liar!" I shouted. I didn't want to believe a word out of Coal's mouth, his tongue was poisonous. He showed no sympathy and the Coal I knew from the first days was gone, it was all a charade in order to sustain my sanity for as long as they could.

"You don't remember the fire when you were a child? The orphanage?" he asked, reminding me of my recovered memories. I remembered the orphanage leading me to the snowflake, and the rose leading me to the fire—my home. The memories cut into me like a dagger as I connected them together. My eyes filled with tears and my throat felt as though it was swelling up, making it impossible to speak to Coal.

"I have a proposition for you Noah. You suffered from a traumatic experience in your life, but I made the pain go away. I removed those painful memories. However, not all of your memories are negative experiences. If you cooperate with us…" Coal said, pulling out a syringe. "If you help us by telling us your dreams and by taking a mental note of them, I will personally give you want you want."

I noticed the syringe was filled with a bright green liquid, "Do you know what this is Noah? A formula we've created to help you recover all of your lost memories. This formula specifically targets the damaged neurons that helped your brain form your long-term memories. I would be willing to give this to you in exchange for your dreams," he told me. I thought about how easier my life would be, how good it would feel to finally wake up knowing exactly who I was.

"How soon can I have it?" I asked. "What about the others? When will you free us from this place?" I continued. I had so many questions, and my patience was running low.

Coal pulled out a small black book and place it on my bed. "If you can record every detail of every dream for the next few weeks, you can have the formula," he said. "There isn't enough ready for everyone, but the others will have their chance to cooperate. The sooner you all cooperate, the sooner we will find a cure and leave this place behind." Coal grinned, tapping the book with his fingers. There it was again; that grin that I didn't trust. I wanted to curse him but Violet was right, I had to play these people at their own game if I wanted to win.

Coal summoned the same two men who tied me before. I wondered how many people worked in that place. I had to be smart, I had to work out exactly how many people were running the place. "Do we have a deal?" Coal asked me and then thanked the men for untying me from my bed. I replied with a nod as I pulled myself upright. "Smart choice! Don't let me down Noah!

The rest of the world is counting on us," he told me, finally leaving the room.

The black book that Coal had placed on my bed was a diary, a place to record my dreams as proof. From what I was aware of, Coal wasn't telepathic. He had no way to determine that whatever I was writing was true or not. I could never bring myself to trusting him, but part of me wanted that formula. I decided to tell the half-truth; altering the experiences I'd already had and blending them with my imagination until I created something believable. Every morning, I would plan on filling the book with nonsense—either way, I would soon discover whether Coal was true to his word.

I reached under my bed into the pile of blank sheets of paper, I had to recreate my real dream. My fourth creation was a paper owl, a symbol of the watchers from the land of awareness. When I looked out the window, I realised the sun had gone and the sixth night was finally upon us. It was time to meet the others and devise our plan.

I walked towards the window where I saw the others standing by the tall tree, relieved that they had received the message. I opened the window and walked towards them. "There he is! The man with the grand plan!" I heard Violet shout, clapping her hands as I approached. I was glad to see the other prisoners waiting for me; Violet, Rudo, Aurora… All, except the Asian girl who I encountered the night before. "Oh…she's up there!" Violet said, pointing to the branches of the tall tree, "She doesn't speak any English, that one!" I looked up to see the Asian girl who was inspecting my paper origami.

"There should be six of us, right?" I asked the others. I remembered the sixth window, the last prisoner I was yet to meet.

"Well honey, everyone was invited…" Violet said.

"Maybe they never saw the message?" Rudo interrupted Violet

"Maybe there isn't another prisoner in the sixth room?" Aurora said. Maybe she was right, but I remembered the mysterious person lurking around the garden from before.

"Look, we can all stand here and play the maybe game, or we can come up with a plan that will get us all out of here," Violet suggested. That was the reason we met, regardless if everyone received the message.

"We can't leave a man behind!" Rudo told Violet, "we're all in this together!"

"Says the guy who couldn't even remember his own name a few days ago!" Violet replied, laughing.

"Okay, guys! We will come up with a plan, and whoever sees the sixth prisoner first can fill them in," I suggested, looking up at the Asian girl who looked completely lost in her own world. I knew I would need to find another way to communicate the plan to her.

"So, what do we have so far? Any ideas?" Violet asked. Rudo instantly raised his hand. "Preferably someone who isn't a farmer!" Violet had a love-hate relationship with Rudo. They were from the same age group and I suspected a romance in the making. Rudo frowned at her, lowering his hand. "What? Do you expect us to dig our way out of here?" she asked, laughing again.

"It's a possibility!" Rudo replied. He had a point, but the facility was built around one of the oldest tree in Africa, the scientists were smart enough to consider our escape before they constructed the place.

I looked up the large white walls that surrounded us. I remembered, "The sleepers!" My mentioning of them was enough to get the others' full attention. "Remember how I set them off all at the same time?" I looked at the others' faces, "What If I set them all off again? Only next time, we'll be ready. We'll find a way to get them out here!" I told them.

"Even if we get them outside, those things will put us to sleep!" Violet said, reminding me how the sound managed to travel through the small gaps in her fingers.

"Right, but what if we found something to put in our ears? I noticed Dr Coal was carrying a device that controlled the sleeper in my room. If we can get that, we can control them until we find our way out," I told them. Aurora's eyes lit with the idea of finally escaping.

"What could possibly stop that dreadful noise from exploding our ear drums again?" Violet asked. I could tell she hated the idea of setting the sleepers off again, the idea of experiencing that high-pitched frequency again.

"Your clothes!" I replied to Violet. Her white dress was made from cotton, we would just need to find a way to tear it into pieces—after all, she was a naturist.

"That's ridiculously brilliant! Well my fellow inmates, we have a plan after all!" Violet laughed, gently pushing Rudo's shoulder. "Don't you be getting any ideas now farmer Rude!" Rudo finally laughed at Violet's playful sarcasm. Romance was in the air.

We decided to meet by the tall tree every night until we came up with a solid plan, and when we felt ready we would eventually put our plan to the test. Before we parted ways I remembered Aurora's locket, "Psst! Aurora, I have something that belongs to you!" I reached into my pocket to grab the silver locket, "You dropped it the other day. I've been meaning to give it back to you!" I told her, placing the locket in her hands. "I also wanted to thank you properly for the other night, you saved my life!" I smiled at her.

"No, I just made you see!" Aurora replied, before walking off towards her window. I could tell she was still worried about the whereabouts of the panther, whether it had been freed or not. I know because I felt it too. I remember the sadness in its eyes before it was shot with the tranquilizer. Above everything, I was glad I never died a blind death that night.

After carefully watching the others enter their rooms, I added my paper owl to the tall tree. Before heading back to my room, I walked in a full circle, making one stop by the third window. The last remaining window. I wondered if there really was anyone in there. I looked around the surrounding grass where I'd left the message—but it was gone.

Chapter Twenty-One
Into the Fire

I checked the area over, making sure I hadn't accidently missed it. Before I knew it, my curiosity got the better of me, again. I found myself getting closer to the window. I noticed the window had been left slightly open. There was no light inside, just a dark opening, "Hello?" I said, reaching towards the door panel. I wondered if touching an already opened window would set off the sleepers, especially if the light was off. Before my hand could make any contact with the door, I heard a loud thud amongst the trees in the centre of the garden.

Startled by the loud sound, I turned back towards the tall tree. I hoped it was another gift from the tall tree, a broken branch containing another lost memory. When I reached the bottom of the baobab, I discovered the fourth broken branch. "Thank you!" I said, bowing my head to the tall tree. Maybe that was my gift, like Aurora. Maybe I really was connecting with this tree somehow, the broken branches couldn't have been a coincidence. In the beginning, I thought I was just going crazy, but that sixth night I witnessed the pattern with my own eyes.

I crouched down beside the pile of broken branches and placed my hand upon the fourth. Like magnets, my hand stuck to the branch. I could feel my palm burning like I'd dipped it into burning hot water. "Argh!" I screamed in pain, lifting my hand off the branch. I realised I was no longer in the garden.

VIER

"Ijus!" The voice of the rose shouted at me. But was no longer in my hands. I was standing in front of what used to be

my home. The fire was gone and all that was left behind were the remains—my childhood had turned to ashes.

My house vanished before my eyes, and I was back in the same circle, surrounded by the same ten trees as before. This time it was different. The sunlight had gone and I was standing in complete darkness.

"Noah!" I heard the voice of the rose crying. But it was nowhere to be seen. "I'm down here! Help!" I realised I was standing on loose soil, a circle that had been dug up then filled back in. I was surrounded by strange voices, drawing in closer.

"Komm zurück!" I could hear a strange man shouting in the distance, but I couldn't see any faces.

"Quick, Noah! You must hurry!" the rose shouted from beneath my feet. I could see flashlights behind the trees as the strange men approached closer! I dropped on the ground in fear and began to dig into the ground with my bare hands. "Please Noah, before it's too late!" the rose cried again.

"I'm trying!" I replied, digging faster. I could feel the dirt sticking inside my nails as I dug deeper and deeper into the circle. I finally reached a silver chain, and carefully pulled it to reveal…

"Aufhören!" One of the men shouted and blinded me with the light of a flashlight. I realised the man was a soldier and when I looked back down at the object that I dug up, I could feel a big lump in my throat. The silver chain was attached to a circular locket—Aurora's locket!

When I emerged from the fourth recognition, I fell back onto the grass. Did I know Aurora from before? Were these my memories or hers? Somehow there was a link between us, I could feel it. I was receiving different pieces of the grand puzzle with every dream and I knew I had to connect the pieces together. I needed more—I needed to keep dreaming. Dreaming was a way of not only escaping reality, but escaping that prison as well.

It was late, and I had more work to do before I made my way back inside. I noticed someone standing amongst the trees in the distance. "Hey!" I shouted over. I realised it was that same mysterious figure—the prisoner I had yet to meet. After realising that I had spotted them, they made a run for it, "Wait! I need to talk to you!" I shouted, running towards the spot where I saw them. "Please!" I shouted again, but they were gone. I heard the sound of their door closing and decided chasing them was useless, unless I wanted to set off the sleepers.

Whoever the last prisoner was, they weren't ready to socialise yet, I understood that more than anyone after discovering where I was. I knew that whoever it was, they were probably just as scared of the rest of us, and decided to give it time. I finally made my way back towards my room, ready to get back to work.

I lay in bed for hours, restless, thinking about the last recognition. I ate my way through all the apples that were left by my door. I knew I wasn't getting back to sleep anytime soon, so I decided to use the sleeper in my room to my advantage. After finishing the last apple I threw the remains at the main door—triggering the sleeper.

IV

Before I knew it, I woke up with Aput by my side. "Noah!" Aput exclaimed. Uki was sitting with a flask wrapped under his arms. I looked around to see Ahnah resting in the corner under heaps of fur blankets by a small fire. I pulled myself up, and standing in front of me was the Inuksuk—the great Arctic Shaman.

Inuksuk was standing over me, wearing a white fur robe made from an Arctic wolf. His hood had two pointed ears; one on either side—he was half man, half wolf. Long white hair grew from the sides of his hood, all the way down past his waist. He had a long white beard that grew from his chin to his open chest. I noticed he was wearing a large amulet made of quartz crystal.

"Welcome, Noah!" Inuksuk greeted me as I was becoming more awake. He had a look of concern written on his face. "I am, Inuksuk, Guardian of the Midnight Sun. Shaman of the North. Aput tells me you seek passage into Borean Territory, I am afraid you have wasted a long journey," he told me, before walking outside the wreckage.

"Wait," I pulled myself off the ground to follow him. He walked into the pine trees with a large flaming torch. "I came here to ask for your help, one of Aput's men lost his life bringing me here!" I shouted after him, but he didn't acknowledge me at first and continued walking. "I'm asking you kindly…" I said, finally able to grasp his attention.

"You're asking for the impossible!" he shouted as he turned to acknowledge me. Kallik was right when he said the shaman didn't take kindly to outsiders, but this man was my only hope and I wasn't giving up easily.

"What do you know about the Borean, Noah?" Inuksuk asked, still frowning at me.

"I know that your people are scared, they tell me the only person who's ever met one is yourself. Aput found me in the snow, all I had…" I started telling him, but he interrupted before I could finish.

"A map circling the Borean territory, yes? I know. But how did you find a map for a place that doesn't exist to the outside world?" he asked me, stepping closer.

"I don't know. My memories of the past were taken from me before Aput found me in the snow. The map must mean something. I was hoping these people could…" before I could finish the shaman turned away.

"What is it you truly seek, Noah?" Inuksuk asked. All I wanted was to escape the prison, along with the others. I wanted to get the formula from Coal and return to the life I'd once forgotten. Somehow the Arctic reality was the key to escaping that place.

"Freedom," I replied to him, hoping that somehow, he could magically teleport the others and myself to safety. Inuksuk let out a short laugh before clearing his throat.

"Follow me, Noah!" the shaman insisted, as he walked further into the pines. "These people don't wish to be found. I wish to share something with you…" he said. We wondered deeper into the trees, still lit with the eyes of a hundred owls.

The shaman pierced his flaming staff into the snow and summoned one the watchers. A large white owl flew towards us, landing onto the shaman's shoulder. Inuksuk pulled his hood back, revealing his long white hair, "What do you feel inside, Noah?" he asked, staring at me with his large blue eyes.

Feeling was never an issue for me, I was an empath after all, I felt everything. At first, I struggled to answer. I looked into the snow on the ground, reminding me of blood from the attack. "Scared, confused... trapped..." I replied finally. It felt as though I had a never-ending list of negative emotions. I looked back towards the shaman, who was smiling at me.

"Fear! One of the greatest illusions in life. You feel trapped because of your own fear! You've become confused because you don't know how to overcome your fears, a prisoner of your own reality," he told me. He was right, except the prison was real. "Now, look at this beautiful creature, and tell me what you see!" he asked.

When I looked over at the owl, I remembered the words of Aurora when she told me to see the panther for what it really was...

"A soul..." I replied. The shaman then looked towards the owl, slowly moving his left hand towards his right shoulder where it sat comfortably. He grabbed a hold of its neck then twisted the owl's head—breaking its bones.

"No!" I yelled, reaching towards the owl. But it was already dead.

"Good answer!" the shaman said, crouching into the snow. He placed the owl in front of his knees, covering it with the snow. "What do you feel now, Noah?" the shaman asked again. I felt anger towards him for killing an innocent creature.

"Anger, I don't see the meaning behind killing..." I began, before he interrupted.

"Anger! Well, Noah, being angry won't change the past!" he said, looking up at me. "Now look into the fire!" he told me, pointing towards his flaming staff, still buried into the snow beside him. "I want to use your imagination, picture a bird in those flames, flying into the sun," he said. I could feel the heat on my face as I approached closer towards the fire. I was beginning to lose faith in the shaman for killing the innocent owl, but Aput trusted him, and I had faith in Aput for saving my life.

I pictured myself in the prison garden, shapeshifting into a large bird, large enough to carry the others and fly into the skies above. I pictured the warmth of the sun, the smell of the air, the feeling of freedom. "Now, let go of all your fears Noah, as you fly into the horizon. Leave all your hate for the world behind. Let

81

the wind carry all of your worries into the past!" the shaman told me. "Truly feel it, you are free. You can go anywhere, see anything. You are the ruler of the skies Noah, nothing can harm you!"

I could really feel all of my fears fade into the nothingness, like the sparks of the flames, evaporating into the air above. "As you crash into the sun, you become the owl. Reborn from the flames of death. I need you to truly believe it, feel it in every fibre of your being Noah!" the shaman said. I could feel my emotions changing the more I believed in my imagination.

"Now open your eyes. Come, quick!" the shaman said, still crouched in the deep snow. As I walked over, I felt better. The shaman set my intentions—all I had to do was believe. He shifted the snow, unearthing the dead owl and placed it in my hands. Suddenly, the owl opened its eyes, taking flight into the sky above. Inuksuk looked into my eyes, and whispered to me, "The phoenix is born!"

Chapter Twenty-Two
The Imperfect Family

THE sound of the shaman's voice remained fresh in my ears, even hours after wakening into the seventh day. It was clear to me that I had to continue rebuilding my dreams. The owl was reborn because I believed it to be, I felt it with every part of my soul. I had to apply the same energy to the plan. I had to believe that everything we were doing was going to work. I had to feel that freedom so I could be free.

A paper bird became my fifth piece for the collection of my reconstructed dreams—a symbol of the freedom we desired. After hanging it beside the others, I could see Rudo watering the plants of the garden. Violet was dancing around the garden; even though she was a prisoner, she was already free in her own mind, I respected her. Aurora was attracting the stray birds. I wondered if she envied their wings, or if she just enjoyed the company of animals—after all, she was an animal empath. The Asian girl was inspecting the plants, she also remembered her name that morning. "Hana!" she shouted, running around pointing at herself.

"Congratulations Hana, you have a name!" Violet laughed, clapping her hands together. Violet was sarcastic, but she had a big heart. Everyone was in the garden that day, and the plan to escape was bringing us closer together. Everyone had their role in the Circle of Consciousness; without us, the garden couldn't flourish.

I stopped dreaming for days on end. Every night I would trigger the sleepers, but I couldn't find my way back to the Arctic. I was becoming frustrated, thinking that I had done something wrong. Every time I closed my eyes, I found myself enter an empty black void, and no dreams meant no more memories. Even though I wasn't dreaming, I was still filling the diary with nonsense. I was running out of ideas, there was only so many times I could repeat myself before Coal would know I was lying. I counted each day as it passed. There was no sign of Coal, but I was determined to have a full diary of my dreams. I was going to get that formula.

With each passing day, I learnt more about the others. We would meet every night at the tall tree with new ideas. We kept each other sane, they too struggled to remember their lives before. After a week had passed, there was still no sign of the sixth prisoner. We tried everything to get their attention; leaving continuous notes—but they still weren't ready to face their reality. "We'll keep trying!" I remember telling the others. Rudo was right, we couldn't leave anyone behind.

"There's only so much we can do. We can't force them out without setting off the sleepers! You are one of the kindest souls I know Noah," Violet said. I remember Violet hugging my shoulder as we stood outside their window. "Once we finally escape this place, we'll expose it to the rest of the world. We will come back for them with more help!" she told me. I admired Violet's confidence even though I was losing faith in mine. After a full week, we still didn't have a solid plan. We didn't know how many people operated the facility, or what would be waiting for us behind the white walls—we could have been anywhere. One thing we did know for sure, was that these people were liars, they would try and manipulate us to buy into their dreams of saving the future. If their future involved capturing innocent people and testing their sanity, then that was a future I didn't want to be a part of.

On the fifteenth day, we found ourselves sitting in a circle by the baobab tree. We all had our own ideas about the outside world, where we came from, and what we'd do with our lives when we finally escaped. Aurora was trying to teach Hana how to speak English so we could communicate our plan. "I wonder if the world is as cruel as they say it is over those walls," Rudo said, as he sat against the trunk of the tall tree with his straw hat over his face.

"It can't be much worse than being trapped in here!" Violet replied.

"What if we're just as trapped out there as we are in here…what if the outside world rejects us?" Rudo asked. I'd never thought much about adapting to the world outside. I didn't know much, all I wanted to do was find the truth about who I really was.

"If we are as special as they say we are, then the world needs us whether they accept us or not. Whatever happens when we get out of here, we'll have each other," Violet replied. Violet leaned towards Rudo, gently patting his face with a smile. Violet was right, no matter what happened, we would have each other's backs. We all shared a special moment that day under the baobab tree. These strange people were all I knew—they were becoming my family.

During that day, something fell into Aurora's hands—that same unusual butterfly. I could feel Aurora's emotions changing as she pulled her hands closer to her face. "What is it, sugar?" Violet asked, peering over to get a closer look. Aurora opened her hands to reveal the dying butterfly. We all gathered closer to get a look; it was laying on its side, barely able to move its wings. "Oh! Poor thing!" Violet said, inspecting the butterfly closely.

I remembered my last experience in the Arctic from the previous week, my special encounter with the great shaman. I couldn't bear to see Aurora sad, so I placed my hand over hers, covering the dying butterfly. I looked into Aurora's eyes and asked, "Do you trust me?"

Aurora nodded her head, and the others looked at me; their faces painted with curiosity. "I need everyone to imagine they are a butterfly, this butterfly!" I told them. Hana looked more confused than ever, I wondered if she understood a word I was saying. "I need you all to close your eyes, not only imagine but I want you to feel with every fibre of your beings!" I said. Everyone closed their eyes. "Now, imagine yourself flying around the garden, feel the heat from the sun as you fly into the African horizon." I continued, "With every flutter of your wings, I want you to let go off all your fears and worries. Let the wind carry them behind you as you continue to fly closer into the sun."

I joined the others to imagine my own words, gently closing my eyes. I could feel the heat of the sun against my face, making it easier to feel each word I spoke to the others. "Now imagine flying into the sun, feel the flames as they burn your wings to ashes…" I told them. I could feel the vibrations of the dying butterfly through Aurora's hands come to an end. Aurora gasped once the movement stopped, and I squeezed onto her hand. "Now imagine yourself being reborn as the light bursts out of your being, creating your new wings. Imagine you are more alive than ever, feel it, believe it."

I could feel the vibrations in the air; tiny particles surrounding the baobab tree as we changed our intentions. I could feel the others believing every word to be true, and when I opened my eyes I could see smiles all round. "Noah!" Aurora said, opening her big blue eyes. I could feel the vibration of the butterfly beneath her hands, and when she opened them again, the butterfly opened its wings. Everyone stared in amazement and Violet clapped her hands in marvel. The butterfly lifted into the warm air above; its wings fluttered repeatedly, exposing every shade of colour on its unique wings. The butterfly was alive—resurrected by us.

Chapter Twenty-Three
Dream Walker

THE others couldn't believe their eyes that day, under the baobab. We all tapped into something greater than ourselves, we
unlocked a gift; a rare one given to me by the great shaman of
the Artic. I knew in that moment what I had to do to get back; I
had to become the Arctic. The more we discovered, the more
careful we had to be in case we were being watched, we rolled
sheets of paper to communicate our plan into each other's ears.
Before we went our separate ways, another branch broke from
the baobab tree, falling into the centre of our circle.

"Looks like we have another one to fix!" Rudo said as he
looked up the tree.

"Not fix, listen!" I told the others. I explained the purpose
behind my paper crafts that hung above us, and how they were
connected to my dreams. I told them I was receiving memories
from every broken branch that fell. Rudo was envious that I was
able to remember, I could see it in his eyes, and how desperately
he wanted to remember his life again. Upon touching the fifth
broken branch, I received my fifth recognition.

FÜNF

*I found myself hiding behind a large pine tree, my feet
buried in the snow as I quivered at the sounds of a gun firing
in the near distance. "Ein!" I heard a man shout as he fired
his gun. "Zwei!" the man shouted again, taking a second shot.
I was terrified, crouching lower behind the tree as I heard his
loud footsteps in the snow approaching closer. "Drei!" the
man shouted as he fired his gun again, this time followed by*

the sound of a loud howl. With every number, he fired another shot, and a small white wolf appeared, joining me as I hid behind the tree.

I realised this man was killing them off; these wolves. When the man got to seven, I wondered just how many wolves were in that pack. I crawled deeper into the woods silently, out of fear of being shot. The wolf followed me and I heard the man get to eight. I could hear the sounds of twigs snapping nearby as the man made his way into the forest. This wolf was just as terrified as me, but I didn't feel afraid of being attacked, I was connected with this wild animal.

We hid behind the tree, and I held onto its fur with my trembling hands. When I reached into my pocket, I found the same silver necklace I had unearthed in my last recognition— Aurora's pendant. Everything was silent for a moment, and the man appeared. It was another soldier, dressed similarly to the last. I noticed a red patch on his left arm holding a circle with two hooked s-shapes as he fired at the white wolf beside me, "Neun!"

The wolf's head fell into my lap as the soldier reloaded his gun. The blood of the dead wolf spilled onto my white clothes, and the soldier pointed his gun towards my head, "Zehn!" he shouted as he pulled the trigger, waking me from my recognition.

The others looked at me as I woke from my terrifying memory; their faces matched their white outfits, they looked just as shocked as me. Their eyes shifted towards Aurora who was lying beside me on the grass unconscious.

The number ten had a significant part in all of it. I woke up before the soldier shot me in the head, so I knew this memory was trying to show me something. "Aurora?" I shouted, trying to wake her up. I noticed she was wearing the same locket from my memories. Rudo picked her off the ground after she finally opened her eyes.

"C'mon girl, let's get you some water!" Rudo said, walking towards his room. Rudo was the father figure in the circle; always taking care of us, even though he couldn't remember his life. He had a natural instinct when it came to children. He cared for Aurora like she was his own.

I looked around at all the broken branches, then up to my recreations from the tree above; I realised that the pattern was real, and I still had to complete another five pieces in order to escape.

"Poor thing! Are you okay, Noah? What happened there?" I heard Violet ask, but her voice faded into the background noise as I looked up the baobab tree. I knew I was uncovering something big with every memory, and somehow Aurora was a part of that. I had to get back to the Arctic for more answers.

On the fifteenth night, I left my window open once the air became cooler. I wanted to create a cold atmosphere to help me concentrate. I stripped out of my clothes and lay on the white marble floor, and closed my eyes. I imagined Aput, and his tribe, I imagined the snow and the freezing air as I drifted further asleep.

V

"Noah!" I heard Uki shout as I woke up to her smiling face.

"Uki! Where's your mother and father?" I asked, pulling myself up. I realised I was still inside the plane wreckage.

"Here!" I heard Aput reply as he entered from the inner hut. "Where did you go? We didn't think you were going to wake up again!" He continued, "We nearly gave up hope, we were going to head back to the tribe…" Aput looked more upset than last time, I could tell he was becoming tired.

"Why didn't you?" I asked. I could see Ahnah in the corner preparing a pot of soup.

"Because I told them you would eventually find your way back," Inuksuk said as he entered the room. "You proved yourself worthy of crossing into the Borean territory. I told them who you really are!" I looked at the shaman, confused by what he meant. He knelt beside me, looking straight into my eyes, "A Dream Walker!"

Ahnah looked over at me, more curious than ever as she stirred the pot of soup. "A Dream Walker?" I asked.

"You have the ability to manipulate your reality using your dreams. For centuries our people thought they had become extinct. A dream walker from the outside is very rare," Inuksuk said. "I never believed I would ever meet another one in this lifetime, until you came along! The owl was a test; I had to see for my own eyes." Inuksuk continued, "Before Aput and his men found you in the open snow, you were headed for the land of the Midnight Sun. Aput thinks you were lying in snow for days, you should already be dead."

The shaman looked at Aput; who still looked upset about something. "Aput, and his family will take you to the border," Inuksuk told me. "You will be alone from there, it is not safe for my men to cross over," he continued as he looked back towards me, "You will leave tonight, there's still a long journey ahead!"

"I can't ask any more from this family, they've already…" The shaman interrupted before I could finish.

"They are your only hope of making it there alive Noah, my men know the safest way. Nobody knows the north like Aput, the sooner he gets you there, the sooner he can return to his tribe," Inuksuk told me. He was right. Aput had gotten me this far, and even though I felt guilty, without him I'd be lost.

After an hour or so, once we'd drunk Ahnah's delicious homemade soup, we were set to leave again. We made our way back to Kallik, who had forged a fire. He was still guarding the dogs, "What took you so long?" he said, glad to finally see us. Aput walked up to greet him with his nose, followed by Ahnah who handed him a flask of her homemade soup.

"Sorry brother, we must part ways again. We're taking Noah to the border, we need you to go back to the tribe. You will watch over them until we return!" Aput told him. I could tell by Kallik's face he wasn't confident about heading back by himself. "Take the western route back, you should be safe. You've done us proud Kallik, and when I return you will be repaid."

Kallik nodded, and walked towards me. He opened his backpack and handed me a wooden seal. The figure was carved carefully, I could make out every small detail. "Here, the seal is a symbol of dreams! I've always wanted to travel this far north. I know I lost a good friend in doing so, but I got to live my dream thanks to you!" he smiled. I was so grateful to be surrounded by these kind people. I still felt terrible about Toklo, and the images would forever haunt my memories. "I give this to you Noah, I hope you follow your dreams and find what you were looking for." Kallik smiled, and walked back towards his sled where he gathered his dogs and prepared them for his journey home.

"Thank you!" I shouted over to him as he commanded his dogs and took off into the snow. Aput gathered our belongings and placed them into the sled, and the sky became darker as snow began to fall.

"We must go now, Noah!" Aput said. Ahnah had her arms wrapped around Uki in the front of the sled, leaving a space for me behind. I climbed in, and Aput jumped onto the far back, commanding his dogs to take off. The snow was becoming heavier as we left the ground and headed towards the border.

Hours passed and we were still surrounded by the same scenery, an endless pathway surrounded by pine trees on either side. I could feel my eyes closing, and I reached into my pocket, squeezing onto the wooden seal. My eyes finally closed, and there I woke up on the white marble floor. A stranger dressed in white was sitting at the end of my bed, staring at me as I became conscious. I rubbed my eyes with my hands to get a better view and then I realised who it was. The mysterious figure had finally revealed themselves; it was the silent observer—the sixth prisoner.

Chapter Twenty-Four
Violet Garden

I could tell the man sitting in my bed was another prisoner because he never wore a badge of authority like the others. I could tell by that look on his face; the same look I had when I first discovered where I really was. He was dressed in the same white outfit, and before I could get up he made a run for the door—out into the garden. "Wait!" I shouted, pulling myself off the ground and chasing him out the door.

He ran straight through the garden into his room. I realised I was standing outside in the middle of the night with no shirt on. "Noah…" I heard a strange voice call from amongst the trees.

"Who's there?" I called out. Moments later I realised the voice belonged to Violet, who appeared from behind the leaves. She was naked again, and I turned my head the other way as she approached closer.

"Don't shy away Noah, this is the way we came into this world!" Violet said to me. I couldn't look her in the eyes, I felt embarrassed. "I know you don't understand it…" she continued, "Let me show you?" Violet gave me her hand; an invite into the world of a naturist. We walked further into the centre of the garden, way beyond the tall tree. The garden completely dark; the only light was from the full moon beaming down on us from above.

"How is she?" I asked Violet about Aurora, still worried about her.

"She's a survivor, that one! She's resting now. Rudo took good care of her," she replied with a smile. I could tell she felt a deeper connection with Rudo; by the way she smiled at the mention of his name, how she masked it with her sarcastic attitude.

"You know, once you let your vehicle breathe, you realise just how restricted you were before when it comes to putting your clothes back on," Violet said, looking down at my trousers. Violet explained how everyone she remembered in life, saw the naked body as something sexual. She told me that it was different for her, nudity was about freeing the mind, body and spirit. After changing my perception, I stripped down to my flesh to join her on her quest for spiritual freedom. I felt something change in me as we stared at the stars above, letting our awareness expand into the cosmic infinite. I felt what it was like to be stripped of all the material things we hold onto so dearly. I felt what it was like to have nothing but my naked body, and it felt good—like Violet, I felt free.

She was like a mother figure to me, "You know, they say that it's hard for people like us to fit into modern day society. Maybe it's not too late for Aurora, Rudo, Hana…You!" Violet briefly held onto my face then let go. "But for me…well…" I followed her eyes as they wondered to the top of the white wall, I could tell she thought a lot about how she would survive out there, we all did.

I grabbed a hold of Violet's hand and replied, "It's like you said, we'll have each other. We're family now." I smiled at her, and her face lit up. We held hands and stared up at the moon together.

"So, how did you do it?" Violet looked back at me. "With the butterfly?" she asked, still amazed by it.

"What we did!" I replied. "All we had to do was let go of our fears and believe, really believe!" I told her. She turned and looked back up towards the moon. "When we change our belief system, we can change our reality."

I remembered my last visit to the Arctic. I was so lost in Violet's world, I had almost forgotten my own—I had another dream to recreate. "Thank you for showing me your way Violet. I know you will thrive outside of here, and one day you will find your own people," I told her, picking up my trousers to make my way back inside.

"You are my people, Noah!" She smiled before we parted ways. I ran back to my room in search for paper, and carefully crafted my sixth piece—the seal. After placing my sixth piece beside the others, the sixth branch fell instantly afterwards. The baobab tree was becoming more active than ever. As the broken branch fell in front of me, I reached out to grab it. I fell from the branch and plunged onto the grass below—knocking me unconscious

Sechs

"I saw him do it with his mind!" A familiar boy screamed at the woman, the same woman from the orphanage.

"Is it true, Noah?" she asked me, her face painted with concern as she held the boy close. We were standing outside the orphanage which was up in smoke. The whole building had been evacuated, and children were screaming as they ran to safety.

"Do what?" I replied, looking at the faces of the terrified children as they ran towards us. We were surrounded by flashing lights; the lights of firemen as they prepared themselves to enter the building. "Do what?" I shouted, nobody would answer me.

A black car approached, and the door opened. My surroundings changed, and I found myself sitting in an interrogation room. The woman from the orphanage was sitting beside another woman and they began to question me, "Can you explain to us what happened, Noah?" I noticed two men dressed in black stood by the door, but I couldn't make out there faces. "We're sending you away, Noah…" the woman from the orphanage explained with a sad expression.

"Away? Where?" I asked, confused about everything. I remembered the fire from my home but couldn't connect those two events. I wondered if it was me that caused them both. I felt my body beginning to shake as I fell onto floor.

"Noah!" I heard the woman scream in panic, but their voices became silent. I could feel my body temperature dropping; the ground became colder and my ears filled with cold wind.

"Noah?" I heard a familiar woman call my name. As I opened my eyes, I realised I hadn't woken fully from my sixth recognition. I found myself travelling, moving through freezing temperatures, and the familiar voice was her—Ahnah.

Chapter Twenty-Five
Midnight Sun

VI

W HEN I realised I was back in the Arctic with Aput and his family, I remembered where we were headed—to the border of the far north. I wasn't sure how long I'd been away that time, but our surroundings remained the same, except the snow had stopped falling, and the skies were clearer than I'd ever seen them.

"I'm awake…" I told Ahnah, who kept looking back at me. It was still night and the stars were so clear, so bright; I could see the dust particles as they gathered and orbited the Earth. Green lights flashed across the sky above us; ripples of the Aurora Borealis filling our eyes with the mysteries of the Arctic sky. "Wow!" I gasped in wonder, it was the most beautiful sight my eyes had ever witnessed. The green lights danced above us, carrying a powerful energy; an energy I would never find the words to describe.

"Do you feel it too, Noah?" Aput asked me, still standing on the rear of the sled; holding the ropes, commanding the huskies as they dashed into the snow, pulling us further into the night. I couldn't find any words to describe my feelings as I stared up at the lights. Uki lay her head back in her mother's lap—mesmerised. All of us felt something different in that moment. It was like the universe was telling us that we were on the right path.

"What do you see, Uki?" Ahnah asked, placing her fur covered hands against her pale baby face. Uki pointed up towards the Aurora, our eyes followed her hands to the end of her finger.

"A Wolf! A Wolf!" Uki replied, shouting in excitement. The lights had taken form of a wolf; a loyal green symbol of the moon. The wolf ran through the atmosphere before retracting back into the light at stellar speed.

"Here, the wolf is a symbol of light. To understand the wolf, we must understand the energy of its mother—the moon. To appreciate the light, first we must understand the dark!" Aput told me. Aput told me the most powerful message of all that night under the Aurora. It reminded me of the prison; our suffering was a lesson, we had to understand the evil before we could learn to live in peace in the outside world.

The path finally came to its end as we arrived at a large open river; its surface was completely frozen. A wall of mountains awaited at the other side of the river, and the sun sat still in the horizon behind them in shades of gold. "There!" Aput pointed towards the snowy mountain tops, "Once you cross those mountains, you've crossed the border into the Land of the Midnight Sun…"

"Why do your people call it that?" I asked, as we climbed out of the sled. Ahnah was passing around a flask of water.

"Because over there, Noah, the sun does not sleep. Once you cross into the Borean territory, you will enter the lands of eternal light," he told me. Who was I to disbelieve him, even if I didn't understand how the sun could remain in the sky in one particular place forever. I was a prisoner that belonged to a group of empaths, who talked to the trees and built my dreams on paper.

"What should I expect when I get there?" I asked Aput.

"I wish I could tell you Noah, my men have never travelled this far north," Aput replied, before reaching into his coat; he pulled out a large dagger and placed it into my hands. "Protection for whatever awaits on the other side of those mountains. Once we cross that river, our journey together will end."

"Thank you, Aput, for everything…" I replied, placing the dagger into my pocket. I picked up my backpack and we made our way down to the river. Part of me was sad that we would be parting ways once we reached the end. I wouldn't have gotten that far without the help of Aput and his tribe, and nothing I could say or do would ever be enough to repay them.

"We need to be careful, the river is frozen, but still fragile. One wrong move can be fatal. Ahnah and Uki will cross over first, once they reach the other side, Noah, you will follow. I will cross over last," Aput said.

Ahnah held onto Uki's hand before slowly stepping onto the frozen waters. They both moved slowly; carefully making their way across the river. Once they safely made it towards the end, it was my turn. "Okay Noah, remember, gentle steps until you reach the end," Aput told me, encouraging me to step onto the ice.

When I reached the halfway mark, I could see something moving in the water below the surface of the ice. "Good work, Noah! You're nearly there!" I could hear Aput shouting from behind. As I took another slow step forward, I slipped and cracked my head on the ice below.

"Noah? Wake up!" I heard a man's voice commanding me. I jolted forwards out of my bed to see Coal staring directly at me. Coal was holding the black diary in his hands, "I know I'm early, but I see you've been keeping your end of the bargain..."

Coal reached into his white coat, and pulled out the formula. "Except... I know now that these aren't your real dreams!" Coal threw the black diary against the wall. Somehow, he found out that I had been lying in the diary. "You know Noah, I thought we could trust each other. I don't want to have to hurt any of your friends..." Coal looked out the window into the garden. On the other side of the glass I could see one of the prisoners standing underneath the tall tree—Violet.

Chapter Twenty-Six
Paper Snow

COAL was serious about hurting the others; he would do whatever was necessary to get what he wanted, even if it involved violence. That morning I realised our time was up, "You have until the end of the day to tell me everything, otherwise…" Coal told me, still looking over at Violet in the garden. He left abruptly, slamming the main door. I had to tell the others about the danger ahead, and we would need to put our plan into action—immediately.

I grabbed every sheet of paper from under my bed and ran out into the garden. "Round up the others, we escape today!" I told Violet, she could tell I was worried.

"But we don't have a solid plan…" she replied. "We aren't ready yet!"

"Please! Violet…Coal wants to hurt us, and he's going to today if he doesn't get what he wants!" I told her, grabbing a hold of her shoulders.

"How can you be sure? Nobody's going to hurt us! How do you know what he wants?" Violet was becoming more anxious, she wasn't ready to face the dangers ahead, none of us were.

"He came to my room! He found out that the diary was a decoy in order to get the…" before I could finish, I realised I hadn't been completely honest with the others. Exposing the formula would only create distrust between us, and to escape, we needed each other.

"In order to get what, Noah?" Violet asked. "You're scaring me! None of this is making any sense. There's something you aren't telling me!"

"The tree has been helping me regain my memories. I didn't know it at first, but if I expose my real dreams to Coal, he would eventually work it all out," I tried to tell Violet.

"Work what out?" Violet asked, struggling to comprehend at first.

"That the tree has been helping us escape all along!" I told her. Coal was right about the connection between plant and human consciousness; he chose me because I had the ability to communicate with the tree through my dreams. He knew all along that the tree had been connecting with me, he just didn't know what. The baobab was a part of my dreams, displaying itself through various symbols; once I recreated those symbols, the tree knew I was listening, it knew that I understood the message and gave me my memories in return. I still didn't understand completely what was happening, but that I was sure of.

Violet ran off to gather the others, while I sat below the tall tree with my sheets of paper, ready to craft the seventh piece. I could feel that we were running out of time, and whatever dreaming I had left to do, would have to be done in the daylight. I had to use all the knowledge I gathered so far. I had to become the Dream Walker. "Noah?" I heard Aurora's voice call out as she approached from behind, "What are you doing?" she asked.

"We're leaving this place today, Aurora!" I told her, inviting her to sit beside me on the grass. Aurora couldn't remember how she got her locket, and asking her impossible questions would only slow us down.

"You still never showed me how to make one…" Aurora said, looking up at the pieces of origami. No matter how much danger we were in, or what we were about to face, there was one thing I was certain about; I would never refuse to teach Aurora anything. I handed her a sheet of paper from the pile, and guided her through my seventh piece.

"Do you know what we're building yet?" I asked her, she enjoyed being creative; her blue eyes lit once she began to master the origami. She shook her head; completely oblivious to what she was crafting from the paper. After the last few folds, she looked at me and gasped in amazement, "A wolf!" she said. It was as if Uki was sitting right in front of me, I had flashbacks of her pointing into the Arctic sky.

"Okay, now we need to hang the wolf up there!" I told Aurora, ready to make my climb.

"Noah, can I ask a question?" Aurora asked. "What if Rudo is right, what if the outside doesn't accept us?"

"Anyone who doesn't accept you is a fool, Aurora!" I replied, slowly making my way up the baobab. Aurora handed me the paper and string, "You are the most gifted person I know, don't ever forget that!" I told her, finally pulling myself up onto the branch of the tree. After hanging the wolf, we waited for the others to join us. After I climbed back down, I realised the tree stopped responding. I circled the tree, waiting for another branch to fall but nothing broke. I thought that maybe I was doing something wrong? Maybe the wolf was the wrong symbol? I asked myself what I had missed from the last experience in the Arctic.

I started replaying every moment over in my head; from waking up in the beginning all the way to the frozen river. "What's wrong, Noah?" Aurora asked, she could tell I was becoming frustrated, waiting for the tree to respond. I remembered the mountain, and quickly began to craft another piece of paper. The others finally arrived; Violet was out of breath, and both Hana and Rudo looked more confused than ever.

"Violet tells us we're in some kind of trouble?" Rudo asked, he was carrying a small garden shovel in his right hand.

"Rudo! Where did you get that shovel?" I asked. I remembered the first time I saw Rudo; he was carrying a watering can.

"From my room…when I first woke up in this place, I found farming tools beneath my bed. Why? What's wrong?" he asked, then it clicked; we were all different types of empaths, each of us equipped with specific tools to fulfil our purpose in the garden.

"I need you all to go back to your rooms!" I told them, "Grab everything you can find from under your beds and bring them back to the tree!" Violet was already exhausted! Everyone ran off in separate directions except her, "Violet?" I asked.

She looked at me and laughed, "I'm the naturist remember? I didn't have anything under my bed when I woke up…"

"Okay, then you can help me here! I need you to thread this!" I told her, handing her my finished paper mountain.

"You know, you have a real talent when it comes to this… I was never good at art myself," Violet told me, admiring the mountain.

"Violet! Please…" I said, handing her the roll of string. I grabbed another sheet of paper, and began to construct the white bear that killed Toklo. The memories of the attack were still vivid in my mind, and the thought of the bear still frightened me, but we were running out of time.

"Oh, a bear! Very nice Noah!" I could hear Violet talking in my ear as I tried hard to concentrate. Violet was skilled at remaining calm, she masked her fear with the same attitude she used to mask her admiration for Rudo, even though I could tell that deep down she was just as scared as the rest of us. The others finally arrived, throwing their findings into a pile by the broken branches. Rudo had various tools used for farming; Hana had tools for mixing, I guessed she was there to produce herbal medicines from the natural resources of the garden. Aurora came up empty handed; she held her silver necklace tight, "What's the matter sugar? You didn't find anything?" Violet asked. Aurora shook her head. I knew her gifts; I'd witnessed them with my own eyes when she saved my life. The necklace she was holding also played a very important role; something that connected us, a secret I had yet to uncover.

After creating the bear, I knew there was one last piece I had to create. Something was missing; I tried to think about the creature swimming under the frozen river. "I need you guys to help me think here, think of creatures that swim in icy waters!" I said, hoping they could help me complete another piece. Everyone tried to think, but couldn't remember all the different kinds of animals from the outside world—everyone but Aurora.

Aurora stepped forward. "I had a dream last night… I was on the back of a whale sailing through cold water," she told me. My intuition was telling me to listen to her, and if we were connected somehow, then maybe Aurora's dream was the last missing piece. I quickly constructed a whale before gathering the other two pieces. I was running out of hope and time, and I knew that if the tree didn't respond, we would have to come up with another plan.

"Careful!" Violet said as I climbed up the tree with the final pieces. When it came to attaching the last piece, I closed my eyes in hope of something magical happening. "Well?" I could hear Rudo shout from the ground below. Nothing happened; I could feel the last of my hope slipping away. I didn't want to tell the others that I never had a back-up plan.

"Please!" I prayed quietly to the tree. I could feel the hands of time ticking with every passing moment. It was time to give up on my dreams, and think of another plan to escape. I slowly climbed back down the tree to join the others who were waiting patiently at the bottom—waiting for my answer.

"I'm sorry guys…" I apologised. I couldn't bear to look at Aurora; the thought of disappointing a child, killed me inside. All I wanted was to get everyone out so they could experience life and rediscover who they really were. In that moment of silence, the remaining four branches dropped from the baobab onto the ground behind me. Before I could even think about touching them, Rudo's face dropped as he pointed at the wall around us, it was the same square that appeared from the beginning.

Violet cursed, "They're going to reset the circle!" Everyone looked at each other in fear, and Aurora grabbed a hold of my arm.

"All prisoners return to their rooms immediately!" A voice from the device commanded us, "I repeat, immediately!"

"We have to do this now guys, I need you all to be brave!" I told the others, "Violet, it's time to…be you," I told her. Violet knew what she had to do and ripped off her dress. Rudo picked up the garden shears from the pile and began to cut the dress into small pieces; enough for everyone's ears.

"Prisoners have exactly ten seconds to return to them rooms. If prisoners haven't returned, the circle will be reset!" The device warned us. I knew I had to use everything I had learnt so far.

Both Rudo and Violet panicked when they realised there wasn't even enough time to finish cutting the fabric for our ears. Everyone felt defeated, "They have beaten us!" Violet said, shaking her head as the voice from the device began its countdown. Aurora covered her ears and bowed her head, preparing herself for the sound that was about to come.

That moment of fear changed; that same unique butterfly we'd resurrected had reappeared, descending from the sky onto Hana's head. That was it! How could I have been this blind all along? I knew what we had to do—become the butterfly.

"Everyone, join hands and form a circle!" I shouted, "I need you all to believe more than you ever have! We are all powerful, we will not be defeated by these people!" Everyone grabbed a hold of each other's hands and we created a circle underneath the baobab tree. "We are no longer caterpillars, it's time to become butterflies! I need you all to move clockwise, gradually moving faster and faster. With every step, I want you to push all the fear you've ever known from this place outside of the circle!"

"Seven... Six..." The voice continued the countdown. We began to move clockwise, moving faster and faster.

"Our ears will become soundproof; no sound shall enter our circle! We are butterflies, we are powerful...we are free!" I continued to shout. I could feel the others believe every word; smiles grew the faster we moved. Our lives changed forever in that moment, and when the voice finished its countdown, there was no sound—we had become butterflies.

When we finally let go, we all fell backwards onto the grass. We broke the circle but we never broke our belief. "It worked, Noah!" Aurora shouted in laughter as we lay on the ground staring up at the baobab tree. The leaves of the tall tree came to life, like our energy had created a gust of wind. I felt something change inside; we all did. We finally believed in ourselves—we were free.

The wind blew stronger, disconnecting all of the paper origami from the branches of the baobab. All the paper pieces sailed through the wind; falling towards us like a shower of dreams coming to life. "Would you look at that!" Rudo said as they descended closer to the ground.

"Your dreams are finally blossoming, Noah!" I heard Violet, clapping in amazement.

Aurora turned towards me, those big blue oceans came to life, I could almost see the life swimming through them. She smiled then said, "It's paper snow!"

Chapter Twenty-Seven
Attack of the Sleepers

W E lay still in the grass until the paper snow finally stopped. The pieces had finally landed around us, "What now?" Violet asked. We knew that we still had to escape the prison, but we felt untouchable in that moment. I turned towards my room where I saw Coal standing by the door to the garden with a device in his hand. His face was in disbelieve; he had come to switch off the sleepers, expecting us to be asleep, but we were awake—wide awake.

"We wait for them to come to us!" I replied. We all helped each other off the ground and security stepped into the garden from each room, circling us. "Don't worry, they don't have sound proof ears like us. We need to get that remote from Coal."

I looked around, remembering that every room had a trigger whenever an unauthorised empath tried to enter. "Everyone, pick someone else's room and run towards it, we need to distract these men. Aurora, I need you to run towards mine as fast as you can!" I told her, "And remember, when we trigger the sleepers, remember just how powerful you all are!" Everyone ran to a separate room; Aurora and I ran towards mine. "Don't stop running until you reach the entrance!" I shouted to Aurora before we approached Coal.

Coal knew our plan and reached out towards Aurora, pulling her to the ground. Coal dodged out of the way before I could run into him. Aurora screamed as they fell to the ground, "Noah!" I ran up behind him and pulled him off, falling backwards as he tried to wrestle me off. Aurora looked up, trying to pick herself off the ground.

"Go Aurora!" I shouted. Coal had dropped the device beside him on the grass, but before I could grab it he threw his hands around my neck. He choked me as hard as he could until I began to slip in and out of consciousness. I kept seeing constant flashes of Ahnah dragging me through the ice; she was trying to pull me to the other side of the frozen river. I could see Aput wrestling with a bear in the distance, the same bear that killed Toklo. Aput fell to the ground and the bear came running towards us!

"Noah, wake up! Please!" Ahnah screamed, still dragging me across the frozen river as the bear approached closer with its blood-stained mouth.

"I'm sorry Noah, but you left me no choice!" I heard Coal talking through his teeth as he used all this strength to put an end to me. In that moment, blood started dripping onto Coal's face from his ears and he finally let go. His eyes closed and he fell head first onto the grass beside me. Aurora made it; she had activated all of the sleepers.

"Noah!" I heard Rudo shout as he ran towards me, assisting me off the ground. I looked around to see the security sleeping like scattered sheep around the garden. The others finally joined us and Violet picked up the device to control the sleepers.

"How long do you think they'll stay like that?" Violet asked before kicking Coal in the side.

"I'm not sure, but we need to find a way out, now!" I replied, "Check all the main doors in the rooms, see if any have been left open!" We all checked our rooms, but none of the doors had been left open which meant the only way out had to be through the garden. After we met back up in the garden, we realised we were running out of ideas.

"There's no way over those walls!" Rudo said as he looked up trying to calculate its height.

After looking around I noticed, that scattered around the tops of the walls were small spikes, built to keep any animal brave enough to climb over, out. "There has to be another way!" I told the others, desperate to find anything we could use to escape. I walked back towards the tall tree where the broken branches lay. The others followed me, struggling to find anything that would help us escape.

"All this can't be for nothing!" Rudo said. "There has to be something, anything!"

"Not unless you plan on sailing over the walls…" Violet said as she picked up my paper boat from the grass. The string from the boat dangled in the air, catching my eyes as I stood there in a daydream. I realised that the broken branches weren't just gifts of forgotten memories, they were our escape too.

"We need to build…" I told the others.

"Build? Build what?" Violet asked. I turned back and pointed towards the pile of broken branches.

I looked back at the others and replied, "A ladder!"

Chapter Twenty-Eight
The Climb

W E used the string from the origami to tie the broken branches together after carefully measuring the distance between each of them. The branches had to be wide enough to cover the height of the wall, but just enough so we could reach each branch. Together we built the ladder; the final step to escape the prison. "We really made it, Noah!" Aurora said, smiling after we finished constructing the ladder.

The others praised me, but I thanked the baobab tree; if it wasn't for the tree I don't think we would have gotten that far. Everyone was full of joy; excited to finally escape and enter the outside world. Even though we couldn't fully remember who we were or where we came from, we knew that we would find our way in life because we all had one thing—each other.

After a few unsuccessful throws, we managed to hook the ladder onto the spikes at the top. The ladder fitted perfectly, all we had to do was make the climb to freedom. "Ladies first!" Rudo told Violet, who looked around to make sure it was okay if she made the first climb. She grabbed onto Rudo's face then kissed him on the cheek before making her climb.

"I'll see you all at the top!" She waved halfway up. The ladder was surprisingly steady, and we all watched her carefully until she reached the top. "Guys! I made it! You have to see it up here, it's beautiful!" She shouted down at us, clapping her hands with excitement. The moment Violet reached the top was one of the happiest moments in the prison. Violet told us that there wasn't much of a drop on the other side of the wall, and that the garden was built into the ground. "This is amazing!" she shouted. "Hurry, you all need to get up here!"

Hana was the second prisoner to make the climb, and before she did, she thanked everyone in English. Aurora was proud that she managed to teach Hana, and they hugged for a moment before Hana made her climb. "Okay, who's next?" Rudo asked. Both me and Aurora looked at each other. I knew I wanted to see the others make it the top before me.

"Your next, Rudo! Violet needs you up there!" Aurora told him, before kissing him on the cheek.

Rudo smiled, "See you guys at the top!" he said. Rudo was the oldest, he was more fragile and it gave everyone a sense of relief to see him make it to the top. Violet hugged him as soon as he reached the top.

"C'mon my little butterflies, get up here!" Violet shouted as she clapped. Rudo and Hana were both amazed by the sight on the other side, and I couldn't wait to join them in that moment.

"Okay, Aurora, your turn!" I told her, encouraging her to make the climb.

"When we get to the outside, promise me you'll never leave?" Aurora pleaded.

"I promise," I told her, pulling her in close to give her a warm hug. Aurora was like a little sister to me, one I never wanted to lose. I had to keep reminding myself just how blessed I was to be surrounded by these people. When Aurora finally got halfway up the ladder, I remembered something important—the formula.

"Where are you going?" I heard Aurora shout as she spotted me running back across the garden.

"Just keep climbing! I forgot something!" I shouted back up at her. I quickly ran across the garden towards Coal; he was still lying face down on the grass. I turned him over to search his pockets for the formula. Inside the first pocket was a pen; the very same pen I found in the garden all those weeks ago. I threw the pen across the garden and searched his right-hand pocket where I found the formula, "You know, Coal, I used to think we could trust each other too, but I'm glad I didn't!" I whispered in his ear. Coal was still unconscious, finally he was getting a taste of his own medicine.

I hid the formula in my pocket and ran back towards the ladder to see that Aurora was finally at the top. "C'mon, Noah!" I heard her shout as I approached the bottom of the ladder.

"Coming!" I shouted back up before making my climb. When the others had constructed the ladder, I had forgotten to collect the memories from the remaining branches. The second branch contained the seventh memory.

Sieben

"Noah, I need you to remember the fire!" a strange man told me, I noticed he was wearing a white lab coat. There was a device attached to my head, and he was noting my behaviour like I was some kind of experiment. "How did you start the fire? With your thoughts?" the man asked me. The machine by the table was recording my body temperatures, and I could see the dials moving all the way to max.

I remembered the orphanage; how I stood in front of the fireplace, I was angry about something. "Are you okay?" a strange boy asked as he entered the room. I remember being so angry about the fire which destroyed my home. It wasn't an accident, there was something bigger behind it. The fire grew bigger, eventually expanding outside the fireplace and catching the walls surrounding it. "Help!" the boy shouted, running out the room. I heard the screams of all the desperate orphans as they tried to escape.

I woke up back in front of the strange man in the interrogation room. "Control yourself, Noah!" the man shouted, as he shouted for assistance. The machine began to melt and the room filled with smoke!

"Noah!" I heard Aurora shout down from the top of the wall. I continued my climb up the ladder, but another memory awaited on the fifth branch as I climbed higher.

Acht

"I'm taking you to a very special place, Noah!" a man told me as I looked out the plane window. "There are others just like you there!"

"Like me?" I asked turning around to see a man dressed in black, wearing black sunglasses.

The man removed his sunglasses, "Gifted!" he replied, as the man revealed his deep black eyes. I recognised them—it was Dr Coal.

"Noah! Are you okay?" I heard Violet shout down. "I'm going down there!" I heard her tell the others.

"I'll go, the ladder will take my weight!" I heard Aurora reply.

"No guys! I'm fine, I promise. I'm nearly there!" I shouted up at them, hoping they would stay at the top of the wall. I felt better knowing that they were up there together. When I reached the seventh branch, I received my ninth recognition.

Neun

"We will create ten guardians to protect it!" The voice of the rose finally retuned as I buried the silver locket that belonged to Aurora. Every day I created a paper wolf; one for each tree that formed a circle in the middle of the Swedish forest. Before I could create the tenth wolf, something happened, my family were murdered in a house fire.

I saw myself standing before three graveyards; one was of my mother, I could see a photo of her face placed on the gravestone and her name engraved on the stone. Beside my mother was my father... "We couldn't find a record of his family, there's no trace of other relatives. We need to send him someplace he will be looked after until he's old enough..." I heard the voices of strangers discuss where I would go after that moment. Before I could look at the third grave, I became conscious again.

"Noah! Please, let us help you!" I heard Rudo shout down. The others were becoming desperate for me to reach the top. As I finally made it up last branches, Aurora reached down to give me her hands.

"You're nearly there Noah! Reach for my hand!" Aurora said as she stretched her fingers towards me, Rudo was holding onto her legs. My last recognition came to me when I touched the ninth branch; the most powerful of all. I was losing my grip.

Zehn

I had finally remembered who I was. The events of my life played backwards in perfect sequence, and every recognition finally made sense. Before Coal erased my memory, he brought me to the Circle of Consciousness from the interrogation room after the accident at the orphanage. "There are others just like you!" Coal said. I had already met the prisoners before, when I first arrived as a child. The only thing that didn't make sense was; I was the same age as Aurora when we first met.

The Circle of Consciousness made us plant everything around the baobab tree, which had been there for thousands of years. They had all of the prisoners, including myself, at gun point whilst we planted food in the garden with full memory of our lives. After we finally created the garden with our memories, the Circle of Consciousness erased them—all of them. They forced us to survive on the food we had planted. If we could remember our memories, they could prove the connection between plant and human consciousness.

Coal needed extraordinary people. People who already had a strong connection with nature, empaths who were unaffected by the outside world—us. He was interested in my dreams because he was trying so desperately to see if I could remember my life by eating from the garden.

Before the orphanage, my entire family was killed in a house fire; a deliberate accident caused by members of the Circle of Consciousness. I was supposed to be in that fire; the night before I created the tenth wolf. "Uppfuttning, Renhet, Balans, Ijus, Rytm, Drömmar, Medvetenhet, Visdom, Intuition and Styrka," The voice of the rose told me; those were the names given to the ten paper wolves, guardians of the circle and protectors of the moon. The moon was a symbol on the necklace I had unearthed in the circle, buried by Aurora during the Second World War before she was finally captured.

"No!" I heard Violet shout at the top of her lungs, when I finally became conscious again. I realised I was holding onto the ninth branch with one hand. "Don't do it!" I heard Violet shout again.

Aurora was still reaching desperately for my hand. I had finally realised why I felt so connected to her before, we had already known each other before our memories had been erased. She left her locket buried all those years, hoping someone would find it. Inside were the coordinates to her home, she wanted someone to find it so they could return it before she was captured. In that moment I looked into her electric blue eyes as I grabbed a hold of her hand; a hand that had survived all those years without aging. "Aurora!" I called her as our skin made contact.

"Noah?" she replied, squeezing my hand. In that moment, it felt as though time had stopped. A loud gunfire filled the silent air, echoing as it bounced off the prison walls. Aurora flew over my head as the bullet entered through her chest.

"Aurora!" I screamed, still holding onto her as she went over my head. We both fell from the ladder into the garden below, plummeting onto the grass.

In that moment, I couldn't feel my body. When I rolled over on my side, I began to crawl slowly towards Aurora. I could hear the others screaming at the top of the wall, "Go!" I tried to shout, but I could barely breath. "Aurora!" I called, crawling closer towards her. "No!" I cried, grabbing onto her arms as she lay still on the grass. "Aurora, we need to get back up there…" I tried to tell her, I could feel my eyes filling up with water. Aurora's eyes were still open, and I could see them move as she tried to find my face.

"Noah? Don't leave me!" she muttered silently, struggling to breathe.

"I'm not… I'm not going to leave you. I promised, remember?" I tried to remind her, but her breathing became slower, making it difficult for her to reply. I noticed her right hand was open, revealing a piece of my paper origami, a piece that she had saved for herself—the wolf I taught her to make.

Aurora opened her hand to give me the paper wolf, and her silver locket, "I was number ten, Noah…" she told me.

"Aurora, remember…I promised you!" I tried to remind her again. Those big blue oceans became still as she took her last breath of air.

Chapter Twenty-Nine
Eyes of Blackness

VII

"NOAH! Get up, please!" I heard the cries of Ahnah; still dragging me through the ice. I could feel the ice cracking as the bear approached even closer. "Stay back!" Ahnah shouted at the bear. When I finally became conscious again, the bear let out a loud growl; so loud it almost drowned the screams of Uki from the other side. The bear was standing on its hind legs, baring its teeth at us; its mouth splashed with the blood of the innocent Aput.

"Ahnah!" I replied, we still had a short distance to travel to get to the other side. "Run to Uki, now!" I shouted at her. Ahnah jumped in front of me; the bear grew tall only metres in front of us before diving towards Ahnah. Ahnah let out a loud scream as the bear gripped her coat with its claws. I rolled over to dodge the bear as it threw Ahnah back onto the ice. As they both fell backwards onto the ice beside me, lines grew where we lay as the ice began to crack open.

The bear looked towards me, staring at me with its eyes of blackness. I remembered those eyes; they resembled the eyes of Coal—an endless black abyss. I remembered everything; I remembered what Coal had done to us from the beginning, how he erased our lives. I couldn't think about Aurora, I wasn't ready to face the reality of her being gone. The bear let out a loud growl as it went to plunge its teeth into Ahnah's face, but I let out an ever louder scream; so loud, even the bear stopped to look back at me.

When I looked back across the ice, I saw Aput laying in the snow; a pool of blood began to flow onto the surface of the ice. I looked back at Ahnah, who was fighting for her life under the arms of the bear. I looked across to the other side at Uki, still crying in terror. "Uki, Close your eyes!" I shouted. I grabbed the dagger from my pocket, and was ready to accept the fate that awaited me. I jumped to my knees, holding onto the dagger as tight as I could, before diving onto the bear's back. "Argh!" I let out a scream as the images of Aurora lying on the grass came back to me. I held my hands in the air above me, before stabbing the dagger into the back of the bear!

The bear let out a loud roar as the dagger entered its body, then it threw me across the surface of the ice. The sheets of ice began to crack from beneath us, "Noah!" Ahnah shouted, trying to pull herself up. The ice began to separate and the bear crashed into the freezing river below. Both Ahnah and I became separated onto our own little islands of ice, barely able to stay above the water as our weight began to submerge them. I saw Ahnah stare across at Uki, her eyes filled with fear for her child. Ahnah looked back across at me before the bear emerged from the water again and dragged her into the icy water below!

"Ahnah!" I roared as they both sunk beneath the water. Uki let out a high-pitched scream; so loud it emptied the skies above. The layer of ice I lay on was beginning to sink slowly into the icy river. I gasped as the freezing water made contact with my body. I was slowly slipping out of consciousness as I lay there on my back staring into the sky—waiting for my end. When I woke up I saw the eyes of blackness staring into my soul—it was Coal.

Chapter Thirty
The Manifestation

"I must say…I'm impressed, Noah!" Coal said as he stared deeper into my eyes. I realised I was back inside my room, surrounded by those white walls; a reminder that I failed. "Your plan would've worked if it weren't for one thing…" I was barely able to breathe; still wounded from the fall. "Our inside man!" Coal continued, "How else did you think we managed to get the evidence we needed?" He looked out of the window towards the tall tree, "The panther…" Two men entered the room, assisting the mysterious figure who had been watching us from inside all along—the sixth prisoner.

The sixth prisoner was really an insider from the Circle of Consciousness, hired to watch and record our behaviour from the inside of the garden. I remembered the pen that I found in the beginning, I realised that the whole time it had belonged to them. Coal explained that he knew about the plan all along. He knew the real connection I was having with the baobab, and that he had all the evidence he needed. Coal thanked the Arab insider in Arabic, before they left the room. "The others won't get far… If my men don't get to them, the heat will. They'll die of dehydration out there!" Coal told me, smiling.

"Aurora?" I tried to ask Coal, still barely able to move. Coal was standing by the window staring into the garden.

"We've taken care of that. She was a rare find…she had been a prisoner most her life; captured from the Nazis then sold to Russia after the Second World War. She was the most expensive investment for our project here," Coal told me. "Sorry, was…" Coal laughed.

"She was still a prisoner after you found her, we all were…" I tried to reply. Coal smiled then looked back towards me.

"Depends on how you look at it. What we've done here has changed everything we thought we once knew, another step closer to a better future. Of course, you had your part to play in it and you won't be forgotten, Noah. By us, at least!" Coal said. "We're leaving, we've set up a new project elsewhere. You will survive off what's left in the garden, once we're finished with it…" Coal waved out the window then immediately left the room.

I managed to pull myself out of bed before crashing onto the marble floor, still unable to get my body to function properly. I dragged myself along the floor to the window and pushed the door open. I could see Coal's men set the tall tree on fire; they had piled all the equipment given to each of the prisoners, including the ladder we had built to escape. They gathered all of the paper origami to add to the burning tree; all but one. A piece I had taken from Aurora's hands—The Wolf.

After the men had destroyed almost everything, they left through another room. I dragged myself through the grass. I could feel the strands of grass breaking between my fingers as I shifted my weight through the garden towards the baobab. "No!" I tried to shout, my body was still in agony and I could feel my eyes closing as I approached the tree.

The surrounding islands of ice were beginning to melt, I could hear Uki calling my name from the other side, "Noah!" The bear emerged from the water and began to swim towards me.

I opened my eyes again, and continued to pull myself towards the tree. During all the chaos, I'd forgotten the secret; I had forgotten what we had achieved so far, I'd forgotten who I was—The Dream Walker. I remembered the owl, the butterfly and everything I had achieved with the prisoners. I wasn't ready to watch everything burn into ashes before me—I wasn't ready to give up.

In that moment, I closed my eyes; I could still hear the faint sounds of Uki screaming in the distance. If I could believe anything into reality then I could stop the fire—I would become rain. Instead of praying for rain, I believed it was already raining. I imagined the sensation of the rain as it trickled down my face. I imagined it becoming heavier; heavy enough to create a flood. I imagined swimming through the deep rainwater—deep enough for an Arctic whale.

When I opened my eyes, the heavens began to pour. The rain became heavy enough to extinguish the flames from the burning tree. My reality was changing before my eyes, faster than it ever had before. I closed my eyes again, and imagined my body healing. I imagined the rainwater healing me; each drop of the rainwater carrying healing properties. With every drop that fell from the sky that day, I could feel myself recovering quickly. I pulled myself off the ground and continued to walk towards the tall tree.

The ground became slushy as I approached the tall tree. The rainwater was beginning to flood the garden. "Noah!" Coal called my name from a distance. I turned around to see him standing by the room window staring up at the sky. He shouted as he began to make his way towards me, "What's happening?"

"The future, Dr Coal!" I shouted back at him before making my way up the baobab tree. By the time I had reached the first branch, the water began to flood the entire garden. Coal struggled to reach the bottom of the tall tree as the water reached his waist level.

When Coal finally reached the bottom, he pulled himself out of the water and began to climb the tree, "Noah, wait!" I looked back down to see him staring up at me, "All this time, I thought the tree was behind this, but now I see it was you! Don't you see, Noah? This changes everything!" Coal continued to climb up the branches of the tree and the garden was filling deeper as the rain continued to pour. I could no longer see the prison windows, and the higher I climbed, the deeper the water became.

Coal was getting closer as I climbed higher up the branches, I could almost see the top of the prison walls. I shouted as I looked back down at Coal, "This, changes nothing!" I imagined the branch he was holding onto, becoming tired and weak from the flames.

I woke up back in the Arctic for a moment, just long enough to see the bear being pulled beneath the icy water. Those eyes of blackness that once made me a prisoner filled with water as the branch snapped; Coal's body hit the remaining branches before crashing into the water below.

When I finally reached as high as I could climb, I could almost taste the air from the outside. The water had flooded the entire garden, and the Circle of Consciousness was no more. I used the floodwater to swim from the centre to the edge of the wall after the rain finally stopped. On the sixteenth day after my manifestation was complete, I was no longer a prisoner—I was finally free.

Chapter Thirty-One
Into the Past

I'D never felt more relieved after finally making it to the other side of the wall. The others were right; the Circle of Consciousness was built into the ground, and the drop on the other side led into the African desert. When the sun finally reappeared, it dried my clothes as I made my way through the desert. There was no sign of the others; the desert seemed endless, and I was becoming more and more dehydrated.

After hours or trekking through the dry sand, I could feel myself becoming more and more tired. Before I knew it, I fell to the ground, taking all the hope I had left with me. I could feel the heat of the sun burning against my body, and a small meerkat stopped in front of me. The African heat was making me delusional. I began to replay all the events over and over in my mind. I could see something moving towards me in the horizon before I woke up back in the Arctic.

VIII

The ice had nearly melted, but the bear was nowhere to be seen. I turned to see Uki still standing on the other side covering her eyes. There was still a distance to the other side, and all the ice had nearly melted into the river. I was going to take my chances; I threw my backpack into the water. I knew that if I made it to the other side then I would no longer need the map. I still had the dagger in my hand when I rolled into the icy water. "Argh!" I screamed as the water began to freeze my body.

"Noah!" I heard Uki calling me name, encouraging me to keep swimming, but I could feel my body becoming stiff making it impossible to swim. The other side was disappearing as my head dipped in and out of the water. I started drowning. I took one last deep breath before my body finally gave up.

As I was sinking to the bottom of the water, I could see a white creature swimming towards me. At first, I thought it was the bear, and pulled the dagger closer to my chest as I sunk further into the freezing depths of the Arctic. When the creature swam closer, I realised it wasn't a bear—it was a large white whale. I could hear the voice of Aurora describing her dreams about the whale, and how it came to be our last piece of paper snow. When the whale finally swam close enough, I could see its eyes staring at me. "You need to see her for what she really is…a soul!" I could hear Aurora remind me that every creature on Earth has a soul. I let go off the dagger and reached out towards the whale, and in that moment, the whale pushed me back up the surface of the water. I gasped for air when I finally reached the top and the whale carried me on its back as it swam to the other side.

I had finally made it across the Arctic river. Uki hugged me as I reached the land, and pulled out another fur jacket from Ahnah's backpack. Before I could think about the climb over the mountains, I heard the sound of wolves howling in the near distance. Uki grabbed a hold of me, and I knew I had no way of protecting us; I had dropped the dagger in the water. "Don't worry, Uki, we're nearly there. I'm going to protect you now!" I told her. Before we started our climb up into the mountains, I woke up back in the desert.

"Noah!" I heard Violet's voice shouting in the distance. When I fully opened my eyes, I could see a vehicle approaching with the others. The other prisoners had found refuge in the desert, and they had come back for me. I was glad to finally see their faces again; I'd never seen Violet so happy to see me. The driver of the vehicle stopped and the others came running to assist me off the ground. "I'm so happy you made it!" Violet said as she helped me into the vehicle.

"Aurora?" Rudo asked, but he could tell by my face that she hadn't survived. Violet apologised and held onto everyone as the driver headed towards the nearest village. From the African village we found shelter, clothes and food. The people of the village aided us for several days before contacting the local authorities who then flew us to the safest refuge. We had explained our story, and after a few days, our story became public—the world knew about the Circle of Consciousness.

After a few weeks, the others and I decided to go our separate ways. Violet wanted to be with Rudo, and I was going back to Sweden. Hana wasn't sure of anything and could still barely speak much English, we felt bad for her. I could remember most parts of my life, Violet and Rudo would have each other so I gave up something worth fighting for—the formula.

Chapter Thirty-Two
The Tenth Wolf

"WHAT does the colour white say to you?" I find myself asking this question to myself as I examine the white paper wolf on the park bench. The colour white had been significant throughout my prison days; white spoke to me in many different languages, and made me feel many different things all at once. White told me that, like snow, we can cover the imperfections in life, but no matter how deep we bury them—they're still there. I remember the Arctic and how long it's been since I was last there. I hadn't slept much after escaping the circle, there was so much to see on the outside. I had somehow become less focused on my dreams—distracted.

"You seem lost?" A strange man approached me in the park. The stranger couldn't have been more accurate. Even though I was free, I didn't know what I was supposed to do with myself. At least in the circle we had a purpose.

"Is it that obvious?" I replied to the him. He was wearing a white t-shirt beneath his coat, carrying a black suitcase; reminding me of a specific member of the C.O.C. He sat beside me for a brief moment. I hadn't spoken to much strangers since I left the circle, but every encounter with another human was somewhat exciting for me. I never disclosed my real name to anyone, in fact I wanted to live a normal life, blend in with society.

"Can I help?" the man asked, reaching towards me with his hand, "Adrian!"

"Hugo," I replied, hoping he would buy the lie. We shook hands and he nodded, "Actually, I'm looking for a particular place…" I explained the forest and mountains before asking him if he knew about the fire that killed three people.

"There are many forests in Sweden, and I can't say I ever remember any fires…" Adrian replied, trying to remember anything useful that would lead me in the right direction. "There is a public library nearby, maybe you can look through the public archives?" I remembered the names on the gravestones from my recognition.

"Thank you for your help, Adrian," I said, he replied with a smile. Before Adrian took off he admired my paper wolf for a second.

"You know, they say that wolves became extinct here after the Second World War…they then mysteriously reappeared again in the eighties, nobody knows why," Adrian told me before continuing on his journey through the park.

After making my way to the library, I found myself buried in books; searching for lists of deaths from the late eighties onwards. After hours of digging through the archives, I finally came across three deaths on the same day, under the same surname. The deaths weren't descriptive, but I recognised the surname from my recognition and had to follow my intuition. Vit was the surname I had to follow; the name that would eventually lead me to the area I had been searching for since I arrived in Sweden.

The graveyard was located in Jämtland, and when I arrived there, I discovered the three gravestones where my family were buried. Everything was exactly like my recognition, and the photo of my mother still remained intact. The second was my father, and the third made me realise that this whole time, the white rose was a symbol of my sister—Ros Vit. She had been in my recognitions the whole time, and my mind saw her for what she was; a white rose.

The memories of my sister came rushing back to me as I tried to picture her with me in all those recognitions. When my memory was erased, I had forgotten her face, but somehow I had been holding onto her name. My sister was there when we created the ten wolves. All the pieces of the puzzle were finally fitting together. Uppfuttning, Renhet, Balans, Ijus, Rytm, Drömmar, Medvetenhet, Visdom, Styrka and intuition; these were the names we'd given to all of the ten wolves.

Every day we would create a wolf, and add one to each of the ten trees. We had found something in that circle when we

124

were children, something worth protecting—Aurora's necklace. I found myself travelling into the forest nearby, searching the Scandinavian lands for the same mountains from my recognition. I camped in the wilderness for days on end, until I eventually found the mountains.

After trekking through the endless trees, I eventually found the place I had been looking for—the circle of the ten wolves. I was amazed to find that all nine paper wolves where exactly where my sister and I had left them all those years ago. Ros had tragically died in the house fire; something I was never able to recover from. I remembered how I was able to make my dreams a reality, which caused the fire in the orphanage. I thought about the other prisoners in that moment, how everything led me to this point. I wondered about the necklace Aurora was wearing; I had given it back to her when we first met, and this was the place she had originally hid it during the Second World War.

Everything was finally making sense and I looked around the centre of the circle where I discovered a patch of grass growing differently from the rest. This was where Aurora hid the necklace all those years ago before she was captured by the soldiers. I crouched onto my hands and knees to feel the grass before laying down in the centre of the circle. I closed my eyes and finally I was back to where I needed to be at that exact moment in time— The Arctic.

IX

"Noah!" Uki shouted my name. We were still standing on the other side of the frozen river, it seemed like forever since I'd last saw her face.

"Uki! How long has it been? Are you okay?" I asked, hugging her. Time in the Arctic was very different from the outside. It was as if time stopped in the Arctic whenever I returned to the outside world. I could still hear the howling of the wolves in the distance, so I picked Uki off the ground and began to scale the snowy mountains. When we reached halfway, I noticed that the pack of grey wolves had spotted us.

I remembered I had no protection, but I would do whatever was necessary to protect Uki. Aput and his tribe had gotten me this far to the border, and I realised if it weren't for them, I probably wouldn't have made it so far. Protecting Uki from the wolves was the least I could do, and I would sacrifice my life just to keep her safe. "Almost there!" I shouted at Uki as we reached closer to the top, the wolves were fast—faster than us.

The air was becoming heavier as we reached the top of the mountain. We had finally made it; we had finally reached the border—The Land of the Midnight Sun. "We made it, Uki!" I said, running out of breath. I looked into Uki's eyes; her eyes reflected the eternal sun, and she pointed to the near distance. The snow ended on the other side of the border; lands of green grew, and the sun was shining brighter than ever. Uki had never seen grass grow her entire life, and was eager to step across. I knew Uki's tribe had a sacred treaty with the Borean, but I couldn't bring myself to leave her behind, she would cross the border with me.

When Uki and I finally stepped across the border, our journey was finally complete. We came to a tall tree that grew even taller than the baobab from the Circle of Consciousness. "Wow!" Uki said, amazed by all the colours. Everything seemed more vivid here, even the smell, the air. Before we reached the tree, Uki screamed and grabbed a hold of me. The wolves had finally caught up with us, exactly nine of them.

I pushed Uki behind me as the wolves approached closer. "Back!" I yelled at them, hoping to intimidate them, but they kept on moving towards us. The largest grey wolf was the leader of the pack, and I knew that one sudden move could mean the end of me. When the leader finally approached, he bared his teeth and growled, and the other wolves circled us. I closed my eyes and waited for my end, I could feel Uki's hands as she squeezed tighter onto my arms. "I'm sorry, Uki," I whispered.

The air filled with silence as I waited for the leader to attack. When I opened my eyes again, a large white wolf emerged from behind the tree walking straight past us. The great white wolf looked directly into my eyes; its eyes were like big electric-blue oceans. I had never seen a creature so beautiful. A smaller wolf appeared behind the leader carrying something with its teeth; the backpack I had thrown into the river. I realised these wolves weren't here to harm us, they were there to make us see. The great white wolf opened my backpack with her mouth and pulled out the dead rose.

The white wolf walked towards me with the dead rose in her mouth, and as she approached closer towards me, the rose came back to life. The withering petals grew into shades of pure white, and when the wolf handed me the rose, I realised this wolf was a stranger I'd met before—this wolf was Aurora.

I opened my eyes and pulled out the paper wolf from my pocket; Aurora's favourite piece of paper snow. I pulled myself off the grass and walked towards the tenth tree and Ros's voice filled my ears as I approached the tree, "Ijus." Ijus meant light; light was the tenth wolf we never finished creating because of the fire. I could feel my heart beating faster the more I began to understand what was happening. I climbed up onto the tenth tree where I hanged the last remaining wolf; the final piece we never managed to create, and closed my eyes again.

"Aurora!" I said as I touched the white wolf's face. Aurora closed her eyes for a moment then bowed her head towards the tree behind. The white rose blew out of my hand towards the tree and from the tree appeared the girl I had almost forgotten—Ros.

Ros smiled at me; it was as if she was happy knowing I had finally completed my journey. I reached into my pocket and pulled out the wooden seal then placed it into Uki's hands. "I want you to have this, Uki. It was a gift, a reminder to keep following your dreams no matter how impossible they may seem," I told her. I turned back towards Aurora, "Uki needs to return to her tribe safely." Aurora bowed her head again, and Uki walked towards the pack of wolves who would now protect her with their lives.

I realised that to appreciate the light, I had to understand the darkness first. I had to suffer in the beginning so I could learn to heal. After that day I would finally heal, and the light was with me the whole time, I just didn't know it. I opened my eyes and climbed back down from the tree towards the centre of the circle.

Aurora was that girl who came to help the Arctic tribe when the Nazis invaded, looking for The Land of Light. Aurora was made from eternal sunshine which meant she would never physically age. After Aurora's parents were murdered, she had escaped into the great white open. People said that nobody could survive out there all alone, but Aurora did; with the help of the nine wolves. The nine wolves raised her, they became her family until a Nazi soldier eventually hunted them. Aurora made her lucky escape and sailed towards Sweden, where she found this place.

The Nazis never stopped hunting her, and eventually they found her again. The secrets to where she came from were hidden inside her silver locket. Aurora buried the necklace before they could find her, and when they did; she was held captive the rest of her life. When Aurora hid that necklace, she knew that sometime in the future the right person would find it—that person was me.

I lay back on the grass with my head pointed towards the sky and closed my eyes. As the wolves guided Uki back down the mountain. I picked up my backpack. Inside my backpack were my map and compass. The compass was spiralling out of control, and even though the map was still wet, I could see the coordinates. The coordinates where the exact same as the ones inside Aurora's locket.

When I opened my eyes again I realised that the paper wolf wasn't just an incomplete wolf. The paper wolf belonged to something deeper than I'd ever imagined; something Ros and I tapped into when we were younger. When Aurora was an animal empath and after she was captured, all the wolves in Sweden left. They left to follow her into Germany then into Russia, and when I uncovered the necklace again, the wolves migrated back to Sweden where they were followed. The fire wasn't an accident, my family were being watched all along. I lost everyone during my journey, but I had found the light. The whole time Aurora was that light waiting to be found—Aurora was The Tenth Wolf.